Benjay and the Magical Bubbles

Book Four

I0553826

Bubbles on the Run

Dale J. Moore

1

Bubbles on the Run: Benjay and the Magical Bubbles Book 4 / Dale J. Moore - 1st Edition Trade Paperback

ISBN 978-1-0689823-8-5

This book and others by Northern Amusements are available in electronic format.
e-Pub version
ISBN 978-1-0689823-9-2

Edited by Maureen P. Moore

Cover by Dale J. Moore

Printed and bound in the United States and/or Canada.

Dedications

Thanks to everyone in my life for inspiring me, especially Linda.

Benjay and the Magical Bubbles

Book 1

A Story of Wonder

Book 1.1

Benjay's Halloween - A Short Story

Book 1.2

Benjay's Santa Claus Parade - A Short Story

Book 2

Danger at Christmas

Book 3

Benjay's Battle

Young Writer's Workbook

Table of Contents

0 Prologue

Throughout their history, Bubbles have avoided human contact wherever possible. Elders over the centuries had dealt with problems resulting from accidental or reckless contact. They had developed standard ways to cover up contact. Often it meant immediate termination of contact, leaving the human with no credibility to their story. On other occasions, more extensive or subversive efforts took place, particularly in cases where encounters involved groups of humans.

The rarest of contacts happened by intent. Throughout human history, Bubbles took action to avoid potential planet-wide peril. Action of this magnitude required approval by seventy-five percent of clans globally. Individual clans, such as Peepers's Bulle clan, could intentionally intervene with humans on a limited basis at a regional level. Due to the inherent dangers, even those types of contact rarely occurred.

That the Bulle clan had recently intervened not once, but multiple times in the life of the machine-boy Benjay and his family, was unprecedented. The latest occurrence had risked the lives of two Elders, exposing them to life-threatening experiments by a crazy scientist with the tools to learn their secrets. Having rescued the Elders and left the scientist for the human authorities to deal with, the Bubbles began their long trip home, exhausted but happy.

Unaware of the evidence left behind, they had no idea of the danger to come.

1 Tag You're It

The sudden sharp pain in his back came unexpectedly in their moment of triumph. Fret didn't hear anything to alert him, like a gunshot. He turned to look at the mass of Bubbles surrounding him. At first, nobody seemed afflicted. Then an Elder, Perseverance, jerked to the right like an unforeseen force struck him.

Perseverance called to the other Elders in the group. The amassed collection of Bubbles slowed to a halt.

"Look at my side, Faith," Perseverance asked the other Elder.

She came close to examine him, immediately noticing a small unnatural red spot low on his side. "I'll have to examine it closer back at my clinic in the Globe."

He nodded.

Then the small red spot flashed.

A mass of gasps came from the surrounding Bubbles.

"Oh, no," said Faith.

"What?" asked Perseverance.

9

"It looks like a tracking device. We've seen the humans tag other animals for research."

"Fret!" exclaimed Peepers. "You're blinking too! In the back."

"Turn around, Fret," said Faith.

"I'm afraid it's the same for you, Fret." She floated slightly above the crowd. "Did anyone else feel anything? A sharp pain in the side or back?"

The Bubbles looked around at each other, all shaking their heads no.

"Just in case, pick a partner. Check each other over."

A quick search found no others impacted.

"Let's get back. I want you to get this thing out of me," Fret implored.

Perseverance looked at Faith, then at Fret. "I'm afraid it's not that easy. If we fly to the Globe, we'll give away its location."

"What should we do?"

"You and I will have to go into hiding, I'm afraid," the Elder replied to Fret. "I know it's not ideal. Hopefully, it won't last long."

"I'm sorry, Fret, but that is the protocol," Faith firmly stated. "I can't simply remove the tracker via immersion techniques. I need some medical tools from the Globe. It won't take long once I return with those."

"Where are we supposed to go?" asked a worried Fret.

"We'll have to move from place to place until Faith can return. We'll pick a rendezvous spot for her to work."

Faith looked at Fret. "It will be okay. Just think of it as an extended off-Globe field trip."

"Can I come?" Peepers asked, keen on the thought of a field trip.

"Sorry, dear," Faith replied. "This isn't the type of trip to have tagalongs."

Fret's mother, Hope, came over and gave him a goodbye hug. "You'll be okay, son. Perseverance is very dependable. He will do everything possible to ensure your safety."

Faith huddled with Perseverance, away from the crowd.

"Remember that old house we used last year during the emergency training drills?"

He nodded.

"Let's rendezvous there in forty-eight hours. I know it's longer than you thought or hoped. I need time for research."

A look of concern crossed the face of Perseverance. "Is there something else that I need to know?"

"I didn't want to say anything in front of the group, especially in front of Fret. He's such a worrier, you know."

"What is it?"

"Your mature skin is tougher than Fret's. The tracker is just under the surface. It shouldn't pose a problem to remove."

"But Fret?"

11

"The device is deeper inside him. I'm afraid that trying to remove the tracker may kill him."

2 *Agents Investigate*

Two days earlier, four agents had taken part in a raid on a scenic dell, the most unlikely spot for the agency to apprehend an evil scientist. Thomas Finkle and Gordon Learner used extremely sensitive electronic equipment to capture high resolution video. The device also took electromagnetic, thermal, and other readings of the raid scene.

Max Killjoy and Harvey Hunt had raised their telescopic rifles. The rifles weren't meant to kill; they contained special GPS tracker rifle cartridges. The Global Positioning System (GPS) trackers provided accurate tracking of tagged targets. They aimed high in the air and shot at a boat. A boat that somehow flew in the air. A boat that seemed to be carried by a...*blob*? A blob that suddenly became invisible. Four more times they quickly re-aimed, firing toward the seemingly empty sky surrounding the flying boat. Suddenly the boat lost the ability to fly and crashed to the ground near the scientist's cottage.

13

Max and Harvey stared at each other, dumbfounded. Had they actually hit anything? Why had the boat suddenly fallen like that?. They returned to their vehicle to activate the trackers; eight traced to near the quaint cottage. This likely meant they'd missed whatever might be there, falling unimpeded to the ground. Two trackers did not appear on their scanner. They recalibrated the machine twice in hopes the signals would appear. They'd only had one of these expensive new GPS trackers malfunction in the past year. For two to not work in one day seemed highly unlikely. But with no visible signal, they had to believe that's what had happened.

Following recovery of the scientist's equipment from her lab, the two teams had alternated twelve-hour shifts studying the evidence.

"Gentlemen," Captain McAvoy stated, entering the conference room where the four agents sat waiting. The captain kept as fit as many of his men, and more than most of the other senior officers. "Tell me what you've got so far."

Nobody said a word.

"Are you telling me that you've got nothing after three overtime shifts between you?" He stared them down. "If so, I can void the overtime."

Harvey and Gordon, the two junior officers, squirmed in their seats, looking at their senior partners to speak up. An adversarial relationship had developed over the years between

Max Killjoy and Thomas Finkle. The captain liked to think of it as healthy competition. Max agreed with his boss's perspective of competitiveness between the two but disagreed with it feeling healthy – Thomas's moral compass made Max sick.

Not wanting Harvey to lose out on his overtime pay, Max finally spoke up.

"We've had no luck with the GPS tracker bullets. Eight landed in the nearby woods. I couldn't account for two."

"You likely hit the boat. The trackers burned up in the crash," Thomas Finkle remarked, a smirk adorning his face. "You're such a lousy shot! Letting you take the shots was a mistake."

Max jumped up, glaring at Finkle. "At least I didn't buy my shooting test results."

"That's a false accusation!" Finkle hollered back, standing up and leaning forward to put the two men's faces a foot apart.

"Sit down you two!" The captain looked at the junior agents. "Please excuse yourselves. I need to impart what bad examples your leaders are setting."

The two junior officers rose and left the room, closing the door behind them.

"What is wrong with you two?" The captain barked at his senior agents, brushing back his graying hair. He took a deep breath. "Now sit down and behave yourselves. Tell me what you've learned before I reassign this entire case."

Max relaxed in his chair, though he clenched one fist under the table.

"The lab results look interesting. From what we've gathered to date, the scientist had studied an unknown life form with some interesting properties."

"Such as?" the captain asked.

"A chameleon-like capability to blend into its environment," Finkle quickly answered. "Useful technology for military applications."

"You want to turn this thing into a lab specimen?" Max rebutted.

"Definitely – what other purpose would we have for it?" Finkle replied.

"What about understanding it, its history, how intelligent it is?" Max asked.

"We need to neutralize it; understand its defences. We have no idea how many of them are out there or what kind of threat they pose," Finkle said, pushing out his chest like a peacock.

"You just want to line the pockets of you and your defence contractor pals," Max angrily replied.

"Captain, I must protest these accusations!" Finkle shouted, his chair pushing loudly away from the table as he abruptly stood. "Once again, Agent Killjoy is trying to tarnish my reputation." Thomas Finkle's six foot four, two-hundred-and-sixty-pound frame looked nearly as fit as twenty years earlier starring as quarterback for the local college football team. He'd established many school and conference records, several of which remained unbroken. He also possessed a youthful charisma that often made people believe whatever garbage spewed forth from his mouth. Except Max Killjoy. Max knew the real Thomas Finkle.

"Agent Killjoy, please keep your unprofessional comments to yourself," Captain McAvoy replied, more out of necessity to appease Thomas than any intent to change Max's behaviour.

Max shrugged his shoulders, muttering, "Yes, sir."

Thomas grabbed his chair and sat back down, giving Max a little sneer in the process.

"Unfortunately," Thomas said, "we didn't recover the sample that the scientist studied, just her notes. Gordo, I mean Agent Learner, and I will head out there first thing tomorrow at shift start."

"Good plan, Finkle," the captain replied. He turned to Max. "What's your team focusing on, Killjoy?"

"We're studying the scientist's logs to determine how, when, and where she made contact with this thing. We'll use that to try to locate it."

"Sounds like a good plan too. Remember," he looked at his two senior agents, "I like the competitiveness between you two, but when you have something solid, you need to share it with each other. Got it?"

Both nodded. Finkle then added a comment.

"I think it's of utmost importance that we bring back this thing for study."

"Agreed," the captain replied. "I'm authorizing another two days of overtime for both teams – I expect to see some concrete results. Whatever this thing is, it's the likes of something that this agency has never seen. What we need, gentlemen, is proof. We need to get our hands on it."

"Dead or alive," Finkle added, an almost evil glint in his eyes.

3 Follow That Trail

Late on their second day of twelve hour shifts, as novice agent
Harvey packed up his laptop for the day, the veteran Max turned
on the tracker scanner again. The new Detector1000 series had
come into service a few months ago. He refused to believe
Finkle's accusation that they'd hit the boat, and the GPS trackers
burned in the crash. He blamed himself for not testing each GPS
tracker cartridge individually prior to using them in the field.
He'd simply pulled the top one from the ammunition box and
tested it – the kind of mistake he'd expect a junior agent to make,
not him. He was supposed to set an example for his young
partner. This time he would check every tracker cartridge in the
ammo box. Carefully calibrating the machine, two blips
suddenly appeared on the radar.

"Harv!" he called out. "I think we've got something."

"Really? After two days? Are you sure the Detector1000
is working?" Harvey moved around the desk to look.

"I just recalibrated it." Max pointed at the screen. "See?
The codes on the trackers match our missing ones."

Harvey referenced the numbers against their logbook. "We'll I'll be … where are they?"

"On the other side of the county. They're really close together. Both must have hit it, whatever it is." He looked at his partner. "Well, I guess you're going home for the day. I know you young guns don't like to work after you punch out. We can check it out tomorrow."

"Tomorrow?" Harvey started, then stopped, knowing his partner pulled his leg.

Max laughed. "It's too easy sometimes."

"Shut up and grab your coat. Let's go."

"Grab the Detector1000," Max told his partner.

"Thomas and Gordon will start their shift soon. Should I leave them a note about what we've found?"

Max sighed. "What did the captain say about us working in pairs?"

Harvey recalled the conversation. "Don't let Max get in your way."

"Really? He said that?" Max inquired, disappointed.

Harvey nodded.

"I see he has a lot of faith in me. But I wasn't talking about that. He said this is a competition between the two pairs of agents."

"You're right, he did say that," Harvey replied.

"I aim to win this competition. This information is our competitive advantage."

"The captain said, 'healthy competition' – I don't think hoarding information is healthy, nor will it help the agency in the long run."

"He said we had to share solid leads. For all we know, the trackers are attached to a drone that's flying around the county. Once we confirm for sure that they stuck to an alien or whatever, then we'll have a solid lead to share."

"I think you're bending the captain's intent," Harvey protested mildly.

"Have they shared any good information with you?" Max asked, eyebrows raised.

"Not yet," Harvey replied.

"And don't expect them to. I've known Thomas for a long time. He doesn't play well with others."

Harvey looked at Max, wanting to counter the argument.

Max quickly added, "If you think your pal Gordon will feed you nuggets, forget it. He'll do what he's told by Thomas."

"I suppose you're right."

"I know I'm right." Max held up his hand, with an accusatorial finger pointed at Harvey. "Don't you get any ideas about leaking details to Gordon because it will be a one-way street. Got it?"

Harvey nodded, packing the Detector1000 into its carrying case. "Let's go, Max."

"Don't you need to check in with your new bride first?" the veteran Max asked the recently wed agent.

21

"Yeah, right. She'll see me when she sees me," Harvey firmly stated, acting tough.

"Good for you!" Max replied, holding back a smirk. "Best to get that established right up front in the marriage." He snatched his cell phone from his desk and his suit coat from the back of his chair. "Let's go."

"Yeah, let's go." Harvey paused, putting his cell phone in his shirt pocket but leaving his jacket hanging on his chair. "You know," he started, looking at his watch, "I better use the washroom first. It's a long drive across the county."

"Yes, you better do that," Max agreed. "Just be quick. I'd rather not run into Thomas before we get out of here."

Harvey grinned agreement and started toward the restroom.

"Harvey?" Max called out to him.

Harvey stopped to look back.

"Say hi to the Mrs. for me."

4   On the Run

They'd received clear guidance from the Elders – keep moving. The two tagged Bubbles zigzagged around an eighty square kilometre area, trying to stay ahead of any would-be human pursuers. Their route took them above human roadways to give the illusion they travelled by car or truck. They'd rested for no more than one hour at a time over the past thirty-six hours. Fret fought the fatigue that permeated every cell of his body. If Perseverance felt tired, he didn't let on or look it.

"Aren't you the least bit tired?" Fret asked, huffing as he paused to watch the sun rise. "I mean, I must be fifty years younger than you, right?"

"Probably more like sixty," his companion replied.

"Okay, sixty. Every inch of my body aches for sleep, yet you look fresh as a daisy. We've flown all over the place for thirty of the past thirty-six hours. Aren't you tired?"

"Yes, very much so," the Elder responded.

"You sure don't look like it. How do you do it? And don't tell me it's Perseverance," he smiled tiredly.

Perseverance grinned back. "It's determination, and perhaps survival. I need to stay alert to ensure our safety. This won't go on forever; fourteen hours more until the trackers get removed. Then we're on our way home."

"Fourteen hours," sighed Fret. "Still seems like a long time."

"I know we haven't spent much time together prior to this little adventure, but I have heard a lot about you." Perseverance thought some conversation might pass the time.

"Really?" Fret replied, surprised.

"I know you're the eldest child of Hope. She chose your name wisely. I know you are a worrier, yet you've overcome that to recently exhibit many characteristics of a good leader. It's one thing to let fear cripple your potential. It's quite another to worry about what can go wrong but plan appropriately. We've seen you progress beyond fear into preparedness. The Elders have high hopes for you."

Fret stared at the Elder, speechless.

"I think we should get moving again, agreed?" Perseverance asked.

"Absolutely, lead the way," Fret answered, suddenly feeling re-energized.

A crisp fall breeze picked up with twilight. Nearing the rendezvous point, the two Bubbles had avoided detection for forty-seven and a half hours. Fret found the inner strength to keep going, with nary a complaint following his talk with Perseverance.

Fret had visited one other house that the Bubbles used for overnight trips to the surface. It looked one strong wind from collapsing under its own weight. No wonder no people occupied it. Today's meeting place looked like any other house on the block. Surely humans lived here, he thought.

"It's empty, if that's what that puzzled look on your face is about," Perseverance said. "We wanted a house that didn't attract a lot of attention or homeless people. It is a shame that humans can't care for all their people."

The Bubbles switched from clear to invisible mode as they neared the roof of the large house. Entering through the attic, they reverted to natural colour.

"Why don't you rest for a bit?" the Elder stated. "We're a little early. Faith will likely come just after dark."

Fret nodded, quickly falling asleep.

A gentle kiss on his cheek made Fret smile. His eyes remained closed, believing himself dreaming that his lovely girlfriend Shine nuzzled up to him.

"Fret," he heard her soft voice whisper in his ear. His smile grew.

"Fret," he heard her voice again, a little deeper than usual. "Fret," he heard a voice. It no longer sounded like Shine's. "Fret!" a louder voice exclaimed. "Wake up!"

25

Fret jumped, eyes springing open. "What?" He looked up to see Perseverance, with Faith at his side. He blushed.

"Must have been a good dream," Faith kidded him. "About Shine no doubt."

He blushed more.

"He better hope so!" Shine emerged from behind Faith. She greeted him with an embrace. "Are you okay?"

"Fine. Good, now," he smiled.

"I brought along a couple of helpers. Do you know Change and Aide?" Faith asked.

"No, I don't believe we've met. Nice to meet you."

"Okay," Faith said. "Let's get to work."

Faith's two helpers quickly distributed sensors at the corners of the attic. With setup and calibration complete, they activated the devices.

"Dampening field," Faith explained. "They will block your tracker signals for a brief time. We'll have to act quick."

Change formed five arms. Using four of them, he grabbed the corners of a square piece of floating cheesecloth. He used the fifth arm to smooth the surface. Once complete, he quickly reverted to round form with only one arm.

Aide lay operating tools on the right side of the hovering slab. She nodded their readiness to Faith.

"You're first, Perseverance." She motioned to the table. "I'm afraid this isn't going to feel very pleasant, and even a little embarrassing."

26

The tracked Elder sat on the cheesecloth.

"Lay down and put your bottom up in the air," Faith smiled. "I told you it wouldn't be graceful."

With her patient in place, she picked up a needle. Without warning, she stabbed his backside.

"Owww!" Perseverance protested. "You could have told me that was coming."

"Would it have hurt any less?" Faith questioned.

"No, but I might not have whined like a baby Bubble," he said, laughing.

Having let the anesthetic do its job, Change held a magnifying tool over the prone area. Faith requested another tool from Aide, holding it up to inspect the sharp blade.

"This one should work well," Faith said. "Let me know if the area isn't numb."

She slowly made a shallow cut along the left edge of the tracker.

"Forceps," she asked Aide.

Faith used the tool to grasp the edge of the tracker. She gently tugged it out from just below the skin. Once removed, she held the small chip high with the forceps.

"Their technology is getting better all the time. Somewhat worrisome, it is." She handed the device to Change. He put it inside a small box. He pressed a button on the box which caused a slight crunching sound as it crushed the device. Change opened the box, dumping out the small metal fragments.

27

Meanwhile, Faith had applied a compound to Perseverance's wound. She watched it heal in front of her eyes.

"That's amazing," observed Fret. "It looks good as new."

"On the surface, that's true," replied Faith. "Internally, it will feel sore for three or four days, maybe more for an old guy like Perseverance here."

"I'm awake, you know," the other Elder replied. "You only gave a local anesthetic, remember?"

"I wouldn't have said it otherwise," Faith laughed. "Sanitize the blade and forceps, will you please," she asked Aide.

"Up you go, Fret. Let me get a look."

Fret moved onto the cheesecloth, which Change had finished cleaning.

"Onto your side please. Yours is in a less embarrassing place at least."

Fret rolled into position. Without warning, he too received a quick shot.

With Change holding the magnifying glass in place, Faith zoomed in for a look while the freezing took effect. She pulled back, motioning to Change to put the magnifying glass away.

"I have to go in, Fret," Faith announced.

He nodded.

She slowly entered his body near the tracker's entry point. She examined around the device, giving it a couple of gentle tugs which caused Fret to wince.

"You can roll over, Fret," she told him. "Shine," she called out to Fret's girlfriend who'd looked away to care for Perseverance, "can you come here please?"

As Shine moved beside her boyfriend, Faith continued.

"I thought you'd want to hear this together." Her demeanor got profoundly serious.

"What is it?" Fret asked.

"This isn't easy to say." She paused to further compose herself, knowing she delivered the news to her best friend's son. "Perseverance's tracker lay just under the skin. Your tracker, however, is embedded quite deep."

"Does that mean the surgery will take longer?" Shine asked.

"It does mean that," the doctor replied.

"I'm sensing there's more to it than that," Fret worriedly replied.

"You're correct. There is a chance that I could do some serious harm by pulling it out," she frowned.

"How serious?" Shine asked, slightly trembling.

"He could end up permanently disabled, or have brain damage, or …" Faith stopped.

"Or what?" Fret asked.

"Or dead," Faith replied.

29

Sobbing, Shine asked, "What if you left it in?"

"I'm afraid he'd be on the run the rest of his life."

"We can run," Shine said to Fret.

"Look closely at him, dear. He's exhausted from two days of evasive maneuvers. How long do you think he'd last? It would end up killing him slowly." Faith reached out to touch Shine. "I'm sorry to speak so frankly, my dear. We must remain realistic in times like this."

Fret nodded, wiping away a small tear. "You need to remove it."

"We better get started. I'm not sure which will wear off first, the anesthetic or the dampening field. Neither will be good."

5 Dare

The mysterious manor on Martin Lane terrified most grade school kids. They'd all heard stories from older brothers and sisters. The schoolyard was ripe with rumours of sinister nighttime happenings that went back years. The Victorian style mansion had sat ownerless for the past ten years. Having only occupied the home for a year, the last owners hurriedly left in the middle of the night, pouring fuel on the fire of prior ghostly gossip. Amazingly, the house never fell into disrepair, sparking suggestions the spirits kept a shipshape shelter.

One problem with an old purportedly haunted house is that it acts like a magnet to mischievous kids. It is a nighttime dare for frightened friends. Many kids had turned tail to run as fast as they could.

Fortunately for Sarah Lightfoot, the afternoon sun hung high in the sky while she rode her bike past the house with her older sister Lauren and her friend Tamika. The two older girls had both recently turned fourteen, almost four full years older than Sarah.

"I bet your little sister's never gone into the old place, has she?" Tamika asked her new high school classmate.

"No, she's still just a little girl," Lauren Lightfoot replied with a grin and a wink to her friend, knowing well her sister's reaction.

"I'm not a little girl! I'll go in right now." Sarah steered her bike toward the front walk of the majestic old house, stopping in front of the half brick wall that formed a partial perimeter.

"Not so fast," Tamika objected, stopping her bike nearby. "It's daytime – where's the adventure in that?"

Lauren looked at her sister and shrugged. "She's right, you know. It doesn't take courage to enter the place in daylight. Your first time must take place at night."

Sarah's grip on her handlebars tightened, her palms beginning to sweat.

"Sssure," Sarah replied, trying to play it cool but betrayed by her voice. "I'll come back some night to do it."

"Not some night," Tamika replied. "Tonight."

"Yes, tonight's perfect," Lauren added. "There's a new moon tonight. It will be good and dark. Perfectly creepy."

"Okay," Sarah answered. "Can I bring a friend?"

"As long as it's not Mom or Dad," Lauren chuckled.

Sarah nodded.

"It gets dark about six-thirty. Let's meet back here at seven-thirty. Sound good?" Lauren said to her friend.

32

"I wouldn't miss it for the world," Tamika replied, laughing as she rode off to leave the sisters in front of the house.

"Which one of your friends has the guts to do this?" Lauren asked her younger sibling. "All your friends are little princess types. You won't get them on the same block."

Sarah knew she'd pee her pants if she had to go in alone.

"I've got someone in mind," Sarah nervously replied. She crossed her fingers, said a prayer, and hoped that someone would say yes.

6   Fingers Crossed

Sarah Lightfoot paced in her room, nervously fidgeting with the cell phone in her hand. She'd foolishly accepted her sister's dare to enter the haunted manor on Martin Lane – and at nighttime to boot. *What was she thinking?* They'd learned about peer pressure at school and how to avoid it, yet she forgot all that when faced with it.

In the adrenaline rush of accepting the dare, she asked to bring someone along. A great protector to keep her safe. Someone that would fend off evil spirits in her hour of need. Again, what was she thinking? She couldn't disagree with her sister – all her girlfriends were princesses. They even had princess names – Ariel, Belle, Jasmine, and Aurora.

Fortunately, she had someone else in mind. It was a long shot, at best. The last two days, rumours of bravery had spread like soap in a greasy pot. Though seemingly improbable, if not impossible, news reports and police accounts verified the deeds of courage. Now she needed to summon her own courage to make the phone call.

The phone rang once. *It's not even a cell phone, she thought. Who doesn't have their own cell phone these days?*

The phone rang a second time. *What if one of the parents answered? What would she say? They must be strict if they wouldn't let their child have a cell phone.*

The phone rang for a third time. *What if there was no answer? What would she do then? She had no plan B. Everyone has a plan B. Why didn't she have a plan B?*

The phone rang a fourth time. Discouraged, she almost hung up when she heard a voice.

"Hello?" The voice seemed unsure they should answer.

"Benjay? Benjay Marshall?" Sarah asked.

"Yes, this is Benjay. Benjay Marshall."

"Benjay, this is Sarah Lightfoot. From home room."

"Hi, Sarah."

"Would you like to go for a bike ride with me tonight?" Afraid to say straightaway what the bike ride would lead to, she left that part out.

"I'm not sure I can," he replied.

She paused as she felt her heart sink.

"I mean," Benjay said, "I'd love to go with you."

"You would?" Sarah replied, perked up.

"But I can't ride a bike. I haven't got my new prosthetic leg. It's hard to ride a bike on crutches."

"Oh," sighed Sarah, then a thought came to her. "You could ride on my handlebars. It would be fun!"

"Sure, we can try. If not, I can use my crutches to walk beside you, okay? I can move fast with them. What time?"

"Can I meet you at your house at six-thirty? We'll get back by eight-thirty at the latest. I must arrive home by nine on Saturdays or I'll get grounded."

"Let me ask. Hold on." Benjay put the phone down.

She could hear him call his mother. Sarah kept her fingers crossed. He could hear Benjay talking to his mother but couldn't make out what they said.

"Sarah?"

"Yes, Benjay?"

"I'll see you at six-thirty."

7 Tracking

Max, the senior agent, always drove the black agency issued sedan. Harvey navigated as needed. Today, Harvey used the Detector1000 to issue turn by turn instructions.

"Hop on the northbound expressway for starters," Harvey stated.

"How long do we stay on it?"

"About thirty miles, Max."

"You've had all the training for that machine, haven't you?" Max asked his partner.

"All twenty hours' worth," Harvey replied.

Max's eyebrows raised. "Twenty hours, you say?"

"Haven't you completed the training? It's required you know."

"Yeah, sure. I got through most of it," Max said. "When did you find the time to finish it?"

"I started with a few hours here and there at the office. It didn't work out. I carved out time last weekend to hammer through the rest of it."

"Last weekend, eh? I envy your ambition, kid."

"What module did you get to?" Harvey asked.

"Four, I think."

"Four? Seriously?"

"I started module four," Max answered.

"There are forty-two modules. How does three and part of the fourth count as most?"

"Do I need to remind you who used the machine to find this thing we're tracking?" Max asked.

"All you did was turn it on!" Harvey protested.

"And that's covered in the first four modules. I also know how to turn it off," he added with a grin.

"How did you calibrate it? That's in module eight."

"I watched you do it a few times."

"What if you need to do something more complex with the machine?"

"That's why I've got a partner that's read the entire manual," Max replied.

"How's that fair?" Harvey complained.

"Some partners wouldn't think it's fair to have a partner that's spent less time on the job than he spent in diapers. Not me," Max shook his head. "I see what a smart, young, ambitious agent like you can add to a partnership."

Harvey felt flattered. "Thanks, Max. Like what?"

"Like reading manuals so I don't have to waste my weekend," Max said.

40

Harvey laughed out loud, realizing it wasn't the first time his elder partner had talked him in a circle.

Max laughed along. "I almost forgot what I was going to ask you. Can we use the Detector1000 to see this thing's course since we tagged it? Might provide some useful intel."

"Let me try. We've got a ways to go on the highway." Harvey plugged a tiny remote keyboard into the side of the machine.

"It's got a keyboard?" Max asked, surprised.

"Module twelve, I think," Harvey answered.

"I'll stay quiet to allow you to concentrate," Max replied sheepishly.

Within a mile of their turnoff, Harvey unplugged the keyboard. He set the machine back to tracking mode.

"It's zigged again. This thing seems to follow roads but is going all over the place. See?" He held out the screen to give Max a clear view.

"It may take some time the way this thing is moving around."

Harvey slid the keyboard under his car seat. "This is the off ramp. At the top, turn right. We'll have to double back a bit on the next main road."

"It's odd the way this thing is moving around," Max stated, scratching his head. "Is there any pattern?"

41

"Not that I can tell. I don't see places of interest along its path either," Harvey added, looking at the device's screen.

"It's almost like it's purposely trying to avoid tracking. It may have more intelligence than I thought."

Max flicked on his headlights. "It's going to get dark in about half an hour."

"Speaking of getting dark," Harvey replied, turning the Detector1000 to face Max. "The screen blacked out."

"Is there a charger for it?" Max asked. "No wait, let me guess – module fifteen."

"I'm not talking about a power outage. It's at seventy-three percent and charging."

"Then what is it kid? Spit it out!" Max implored.

"Our friend is gone. Both tracker signals went dead in the same instant. We've lost it."

8 Surgery

Shine paced nervously around the attic, unsure what to do with herself. She couldn't bear to watch Faith operate on her boyfriend, even if the Elder's expertise were without question. The danger, and the thought of possibly losing Fret, terrified her. The surgery seemed to drag on forever.

The black, new moon sky, further darkened by encroaching clouds, dimmed the attic visibility. Faith's helpers held small lights focused on the area she operated on. Despite the lowering temperature, small beads of sweat appeared on Faith's temple. Change periodically dabbed the moisture away.

"Give me a general anesthetic and some healing compound, please," Faith asked Aide, fatigue in her voice.

"Are you done?" Shine asked, approaching the operating table.

"Yes," Faith said, gently spreading the healing compound around her incisions.

"Is Change going to crush the tracker?" Fret's girlfriend asked.

43

"That wouldn't be a good idea," Faith sighed, injecting the general anesthetic.

"Why not?" Shine asked.

"Because I couldn't get it out," Faith replied. "I got it closer to the surface but had to stop. The chip is rubbing up against some key organs, putting them under too much stress after the long surgery."

Perseverance came near to comfort Shine. "You're going to need to stay strong, dear."

"Yes," Faith added. "He's going to rely on you for the next couple of days."

"What do I need to do?" Shine asked, not blinking at the commitment.

"I just knocked him out for the night. He can't travel."

"What about the tracker? Won't the humans find him?"

"The dampening field is still active. We'll leave the power cells from the lights. You can swap them into the dampening devices when they run out. Hopefully, that will get you through to the morning. By then someone will come back with more power cells."

"And if they don't last?"

"You're likely safe for an hour after they knock out. Then you must leave, no matter what shape Fret's in. I'll have one of my assistants stay with you in case you need to move Fret."

"You're not staying?" Shine asked.

44

"I'm afraid not. This problem is beyond my expertise. I need to reach out to a much more experienced associate in the Vela clan. It will take at least a day to get there and back, likely more if he needs time to research. Anyway, I don't dare operate on Fret again for at least two days. He needs recovery time. And before you ask, Perseverance needs to recover back at the Globe. I'd take Fret there too if safe to do so."

"I understand. Which one of your aids is staying?" Shine asked.

"I volunteered Change," Faith laughed. "His unique skills will prove an asset."

"Yes, the ability to create five hands is quite remarkable."

"Trust me you haven't seen anything yet. He can change into all kinds of things. I once saw him make fourteen hands to juggle," Perseverance added.

"Then I guess we are in good hands," Shine smiled, "plenty of good hands."

9 It's a Date

Benjay Marshall squirted some liquid soap on a washcloth and began washing his upper body. He'd never washed himself this way outside of his bath. Then again, he'd never met a girl after school to do something. And this wasn't just any girl. This was Sarah Lightfoot. He keenly remembered the first time he took notice of Sarah. It happened two years earlier, in line to get on the bus. Not paying attention as the line moved, he kept bumping into her. Back then, all the kids treated him like he was infectious, or fragile. Nobody came near him, and if they did, they politely excused themselves and walked away. Sarah had treated him normally. Not at first, but when it mattered. He could hear her words like she'd said them yesterday – "Watch where you're going, dummy!" To him, she uttered the kindest words. Somebody had finally treated him like a regular kid.

Sarah and Benjay had struck up a small friendship in the year following that incident, preceding the return of his cancer. Unbeknownst to him at the time, she had stopped by the hospital

47

a couple times in the first few weeks. He'd always slept through Sarah's brief visits. His mother had told Sarah thank you for coming, but that he needed his rest. By the time Benjay found out she'd visited three times, she'd stopped going to visit, feeling Benjay's mother didn't want her there.

Benjay found deodorant that his grandparents had gotten him for Christmas last year. He'd never used it. He popped off the cap and ran it under his left arm. He winced in pain, not realizing a second plastic cap with a pointy handle covered the new stick of deodorant. He removed the protective cap, applied a dab under each arm, and pulled on a shirt. Finding a similarly unopened bottle of cologne, he sprayed some on. He smelt himself. Another spray followed. Benjay pulled on his jeans and looked down at his leg. He needed his mother's help to pin up the leg for his missing prosthetic. To get down the stairs, he used duct tape from his room to hold the pant leg up. In the hallway at the top of the stairs, leaning on his crutches, he looked down at his pathetic tape job. Of course, at that second Lindsay came out of her room.

"I hope you're not going out on your date looking like that!"

Benjay blushed. "It's not a date. We're going for a bike ride."

"It sounds like a date." She took a whiff of the air. "It smells like a date too."

48

Benjay ignored her, or at least pretended to. "Where's Mom? I need her help with my pants."

"I can help. Wait here." She slipped into her room. Lindsay quickly reappeared with a few safety pins. "Turn around." She removed the wad of tape, carefully folded up his pant leg to pin it in place. "There!" she said upon completion. "Check it out in the hallway mirror. It looks pretty good."

Benjay looked, pivoting a few times to see it from different angles. "Thanks, Linds. It looks as good as when Mom does it."

"Who's the lucky girl?" Lindsay asked.

"Just a girl," Benjay replied.

"C'mon, tell me. I'll find out anyway, you know," Lindsay persisted.

"Sarah Lightfoot," Benjay blushed.

"She's cute," Lindsay said. "Her sister's in my grade. She acted nice in grade school, but I don't care too much for the girls she hangs with in high school. You know, the 'cool girls'," she continued, making air quotes with her fingers. "That mean group led by Tamika. Though I'm sure Sarah's very nice."

"She's great! Sarah's always treated me nice even though I'm …"

"None of that, Benjay Marshall!" Lindsay firmly stated. "You are a smart and funny boy," she finished.

"Really?" Benjay smiled.

"Yes, really. You're a smart aleck and funny looking."

49

"I knew there was a punch line."

"No, seriously Benjay. Sarah's lucky to spend time with you. You have a great attitude on life. Have fun," Lindsay replied, rubbing his bald head then smacking him loudly, though painlessly, on top.

He carefully tossed one crutch down the stairs then used the other one to hop down while holding the handrail. After a few falls early on, he'd come up with this method. He walked over to the living room chair that faced outside, plopping himself down to wait. Benjay could see the sidewalk from this location, anxious for her arrival. He particularly hoped that he could get out the door without his father – or worse, his mother – embarrassing him in front of Sarah.

Spotting his female classmate park her bike on his front sidewalk, he bounded up to get to the door before Sarah could ring the doorbell. He dropped one of his crutches in the process, the wooden helper banging on the hardwood floor. The sound echoed through the house. Though the crutch didn't come close to hitting him, Benjay grimaced in simulated pain for he knew what the noise meant.

"Are you okay, dear?" His mother came running from the kitchen, arriving just as the doorbell rang. Making sure her baby boy looked unscathed, she spun and flew open the front door. "Sarah!" she said much too loudly and enthusiastically.

Benjay blushed behind his mother, wishing he had a rock to crawl under.

50

"Come in, Sarah," Mrs. Marshall replied. "It's so good to see you again."

"Thank you, Mrs. Marshall. I didn't know if you'd remember me."

"Of course, dear. You visited Benjay in the hospital. It was nice of you to do that."

Benjay stood in awe. By the fact that his mother hadn't told him of Sarah's visits before she stopped coming by, he assumed his mother didn't want her around.

"We better get going," Benjay nervously stated, wanting to avoid any additional embarrassment.

"Where are you kids going?" his mother asked.

"Maybe over to the park," Sarah quickly replied.

"Good," Mrs. Marshall stated. "Stay in well-lit areas. It's safer."

"Yes, Mrs. Marshall," Sarah agreed. She looked at Benjay. "All set?"

Benjay knelt to grab the fallen crutch.

"Bye, Mom," Benjay said, moving quickly to the door.

His mother leaned in, planting a peck on the top of his head before he could escape. "See you soon," she said, then turned away to wipe away a small tear.

Outside, Sarah hopped on her bike.

"I better walk beside you until we get around the corner," Benjay told her, looking back at his front window.

"Your mother surprised me. She's nice," Sarah said, wishing to pull back the words as soon as she said them. "I mean, I didn't think she liked me in the hospital."

Benjay laughed. "She surprised me too. You know that she didn't tell me about your visits until a few weeks after you stopped?"

"I guess she had a lot on her mind, with your sickness and all."

"That's what Lindsay said," he replied, smiling.

Arriving at the corner, Benjay put both crutches in one hand.

"Let me boost myself up. Try to hold the handlebar straight for me." He leaned his crutches up against the nearby stop sign.

He straddled her front wheel, backing up to bump into the handlebar. Placing a hand on each side, he pushed up with his good leg, landing firmly on the destination. He felt the handlebars wiggle slightly, but Sarah kept them under control. He exhaled loudly, relieved he didn't end up face-planting on the sidewalk.

"You okay?" she asked.

Benjay reached to grab his crutches, laying them on an angle across his shoulder and thigh. "Never better. Ready to go to the park?"

"We're not going to the park," she said, pedalling them down the sidewalk.

"No? Where are we going then?"

"Don't get mad at me," she pleaded.

"Why would I get mad at you?"

"I haven't been completely honest with you."

"Where are we going?"

"Martin Lane," she said sheepishly.

"Oh …," Benjay quietly replied, well knowing what that meant.

"You're mad, aren't you?"

"It will be dark soon," Benjay added.

"That's the point. My sister dared me to go into the old, haunted house after dark."

"Didn't your parents ever tell you dares were stupid, and accepting them worse? We even covered it in school." He looked over his shoulder at her, seeing her tearing up in shame. "I'm sorry to sound mean."

"No," she said, wiping a tear. "You're right. I normally don't get involved with dares, but it was my older sister. I just want to show I'm not a little kid anymore."

"I have an older sister too. I know what you mean."

"So, you're not mad at me anymore?" Sarah asked.

"No, not mad. Scared, maybe. But not mad."

53

10 Dead End

Harvey navigated Max to the last location of the signal. Max slowed the car to a crawl in front of a block of older Victorian houses, now dimly illuminated by decorative streetlights.

"Which house?" Max asked, parking the vehicle, and dousing its headlights.

"I'm not sure."

"What do you mean, you're not sure? I thought those trackers boasted accuracy to within a square metre."

"Activated, they are. Deactivated, the last location is less accurate. I'd say the signal went dead within a hundred square metres of here."

Max looked up and down the block. "So, likely one of the three houses on either side of the street?"

"That's a good bet."

"Good. Not too many houses for you to canvas."

"You mean, like door-to-door?"

"Precisely, kid. Old school, or vintage, or whatever you'd say."

"Which side of the street are you taking?" Harvey asked.

"Neither. I'm setting up a command post here in the car. I'll keep an eye out for suspicious activity. You can canvas the neighbours, door-to-door."

"Just what am I supposed to say?" Harvey wondered aloud. "Excuse me sir. Have you seen a mysterious blob that can lift and carry a boat?"

"Perhaps a tad more subtle, like 'have you seen any suspicious behaviour today?' Say you're a police detective. People are more receptive to police than us agency types. And lose the jacket and tie."

Harvey wiggled out of his jacket and tie, neatly folding both to place in the back seat. He undid the top button on his shirt and rolled up both sleeves. "Better?" he asked his partner.

"Go get 'em kid," Max replied.

As Harvey rang the doorbell at the first house, an inside light flashed on. An elderly woman's voice greeted him.

"I've got a gun and I'm not afraid to use it! What do you want?"

"Police, ma'am. I'm canvassing the area for any suspicious behaviour." Harvey flashed his badge up to the peep-hole.

"You're the only thing suspicious I've seen today." She paused for a moment. "Are you even old enough to be a cop? You look about twenty."

"Yes, ma'am. I'm twenty-seven. Just have a baby face, I guess."

"Well, I haven't seen anything suspicious yet, but it's just getting dark. Get lost!"

The inside light went out, followed quickly by the outside bulbs, leaving Harvey standing in the dark on her front porch. He looked over at their car. He wasn't sure but thought he saw Max laughing.

Politely using the sidewalks instead of cutting across the lawns, he approached the second house, giving Max a thumbs-up. Two steps onto the sidewalk leading to the front door, a bevy of spotlights illuminated the yard like a pro sports field at night.

"What the heck?" Harvey said aloud, shielding his eyes. He took a few more steps and the front door opened. An enormous man stepped forward, filling the doorframe.

"Good evening, officer. What can I do for you?"

Harvey took a few steps closer, then thought better of it. Instead, he raised his voice to span the gap between them. "How'd you know I'm a police officer?"

"I have my surveillance equipment linked into Old Lady Dubois's place. Extends my protection perimeter."

"I see. So, you know why I'm going door-to-door?"

"Yes, I do. I agree with her. You don't look old enough to be a cop. Do you even shave yet?"

"That's not really relevant."

"I take that as a no," the large man said firmly. "Nothing suspicious yet, but it's just getting dark."

"That's the same thing she said. What do you mean by that?"

"See the place directly across the street from me?"

Harvey turned to look, then turned back. "What about it?"

"That's the place. I'm surprised you cops came out. I gave up calling a few months back. Thought you'd written me off as crazy or superstitious."

"Well, I am new to this area. Maybe that's why they gave this call to me. Why don't you clue me in. Why do the other officers think you're crazy?"

"They haven't seen them on their visits. But I've seen them plenty of times. Too many times."

"Seen whom?"

"The ghosts."

11 A History of Change

Change was the second generation of morphing Bubbles to grow up as members of the Bulle clan. For centuries, morphing Bubbles (Morphs) were thought to be a myth. Many scientists believed that ability had long since disappeared, lost to genetics and time. While most Bubbles can alter their shape from a young age, they can't alter their appearance aside from colour and transparency – they still look like a Bubble and themselves. As the myth proved to be reality with Morphs found living amongst them, panic spread through the Globes. Sprouting an arm to carry something seemed practical; the thought of a Bubble changing appearance to look like something, or *somebody* else, frightened other Bubbles, especially Elders. How could they control these Bubbles? Though crime almost didn't exist, what if a Morph impersonated someone to commit a crime? How would they prove who did or didn't do it?

This unfounded and unproven concern led to horrible outcomes. A couple of clans imprisoned Morphs to perform scientific research to find out what made them different. Other clans focused on the detection of Morphs since they could easily disguise themselves. This research caused much pain and suffering amongst the Morphs. Following development of detection methods, each Globe's Elders rounded up all the Morphs – except the Bulle Globe. Mortified at a looming vote to banish or exterminate the Morphs, the Bulle clan volunteered to take all the Morphs as their own citizens.

The approximately three hundred Morphs found across other Globes were captured like criminals and transported to the Bulle home Globe. The Bulle welcomed them, ensuring they all had good housing and jobs. Some Bulle had concerns initially, but not for long. The Morphs worked hard to prove they belonged and could be trusted like anyone else. They notified others ahead of morphing, using the powers in positive ways to contribute.

Twenty years had passed. Most Bulle didn't think twice about the Morphs. Most Bubbles had one or more special gifts, and the Bulle treated morphing as just another ability. All clans had agreed to relax their restrictions to allow visiting Morphs, if escorted by a Bulle Elder. A small group of clans had opposed, but went along, reluctantly, with the majority. The Morphs deemed it best not to visit those clans.

Change grew up aware that he was different. He never felt punished for it. His parents instilled a great sense of humour. His classmates loved watching his impersonations. He'd worked hard in front of a mirror to get them just right. He practised spontaneous imitations of images from books. After graduation, he didn't have as many opportunities to show off his craft. He still practised morphing regularly, occasionally putting on a show for close friends in his home.

Ahead of this assignment his parents had a frank discussion with him.

"We know you've never gone off-Globe, aside from a couple of school field trips," his father said.

"And there is very little chance you'll run into another clan," his mother added. "But you need to be aware that prejudices linger in the closed minds and hearts of some other clan members."

Change nodded.

"Do you know why your father and I named you Change?" His mother looked in his eyes and smiled.

"I assumed it's because I can change my form," Change replied.

"Your name comes from our belief that you will change the minds of others outside the Bulle about Morphs. You will act as the agent of change, with your attitude, actions, and bravery."

Change let out a slight chuckle. "That's a lot to put on one person, isn't it?"

His father smiled. "We don't mean you'll do it alone. You will become part of the change. You can look to Elder Faith to protect and guide you on this mission should something unforeseen occur," his father stated. "She is very wise and creative."

"Yes, Father," Change replied.

"And above all, son," his mother gently touched his side, "your abilities are a blessing. You should use them without hesitation if needed."

12 A Haunting We Will Go

Sarah slowed the bike going around the corner to Martin Lane. Benjay felt relief that they would soon stop. He could feel her trembling hands on the handlebar, worrying him that he'd fall off. Coming to a complete stop after straightening the bike, she planted her feet to allow Benjay to set up his crutches and hop off. In the rapidly approaching darkness, they made out the outline of Sarah's sister and friend waiting under the dim streetlight in front of the spooky manor.

Sarah dismounted her bike to stand beside Benjay. She grabbed his hand, squeezing it tightly. Benjay happily winced.

"Here we are," Sarah said.

"Here we are," Benjay echoed. "Who's that with your sister?"

"Tamika. Her new best friend at high school."

"Okay, let's go," Benjay bravely stated, remembering what Lindsay had said about Tamika.

"Do we have to?" Sarah questioned.

"That's up to you. I told you that I don't believe in dares. I'm sure your sister will get over it if you don't go. She'll bug you for a few days, then forget about it."

"That's the point," Sarah said. "You have a big sister too. Don't you want to be like her?"

"She's a girl, so not really."

Sarah laughed. "You know what I mean. Don't you want to impress her? Show her that you're not a kid anymore?"

"Sometimes, but I know I'm different," Benjay said. "I'll never outrun or out jump Lindsay. No matter how hard I try, I know it won't happen. I'm good with that. A few days ago, I never thought I'd walk again, let alone ride on the handlebars of a pretty girl's …" Benjay blushed.

"You're pretty smart for a kid who hardly goes to school," Sarah replied, now her turn to blush. "I mean, I know it wasn't your choice to miss school or anything."

"It's okay. You're right. I have missed a lot of school. I missed a lot of things in the hospital. Why don't we go check out this haunted house? I could use some excitement."

"Thanks, Benjay."

They bravely started toward the two older girls waiting under the dim streetlight in front of the mysterious manor.

"If you get scared, you can hold my hand," Benjay said.

"Thanks," Sarah replied. "So," she said grinning at him, "you think I'm pretty?"

13 Mystery

At the request of Harvey, Max had joined him on the sidewalk in front of the extremely well illuminated house on Martin Lane. Having heard accounts of the unexplained noises and visions from the opposite side of the road, they thanked the burly man for the information before going back to their car.

"So, Harvey," Max said, "what do you think of Mr. Tucker's information?"

"Sounds like a bunch of poppycock," Harvey replied.

"Poppycock? I didn't know guys your age used the word poppycock," Max teased his young partner.

Harvey ignored him. "I mean seriously … lights going off and on at all times of night, chilling winds coming across the street, eerie noises? I think he's nuts."

"Didn't you take some psychology courses in university?" Max asked, rhetorically. "And 'nuts' is the professional analysis that you come up with?"

"I didn't want to sound arrogant by rattling off a list of possible psychoses that he may suffer from. Thought 'nuts' suited your vocabulary," he smirked.

"Thanks for dumbing it down for me," Max replied. "I take it you're not a believer in the occult or spirit world."

"Why, are you?"

"I played with a Ouija board as a kid, if you know what that is. That's about as far as I've dabbled. I do believe there exist things in this world that defy explanation," Max said.

"Do you think that's what we're talking about here?"

"Likely not. Most of these 'nuts,' as you poetically stated, don't look for the logical explanations for weird phenomenon."

"Enlighten me, Max."

"Eerie noises could come from buzzing streetlights about to die, the sound amplified by the quiet on this street."

The brilliant lights of Mr. Tucker's house shut down in unison, leaving the agents temporarily blinded by the ensuing darkness.

"I'd hate to be his neighbour!" Max remarked.

"Are we going to investigate the place?"

"Let's call it in first," Max cautioned. "See who owns this place, for one. Find out if Mr. Tucker has any prior convictions. Check out his mental health history – perhaps he's had a relapse."

66

Having called it in and waiting for the information to come back to their dashboard computer, they sat quietly observing the neighbourhood. Two teenage girls stopped their bikes in front of the dimly lit mansion. The agents could see the girls chatting. From their distance they couldn't make out anything they said, only the occasional high-pitched laughter from one of them. The two teens appeared to wait for someone.

"I'm going to keep an eye on those kids," Harvey stated. "They look like they're planning mischief."

"Yeah, they look like hardened criminals," Max chuckled.

"Hardened criminals have to start somewhere," Harvey defended himself.

"Sure, kid. You keep an eye on them. They may use their shrink ray on the house to take it with them in their pocket."

"I'm just saying . . ." Harvey started to say. Max cut him off.

"Relax, kid. I'm watching them." He paused. "And the two approaching kids down the block."

The partners sat in silence. Max looked over at Harvey.

"What's eating at you, kid? You look like your brain is constipated – blurt it out."

"It's Thomas," Harvey answered. "What's up with you two? What's the history there?"

"It's a long story," Max sighed.

"You tell me to blurt out what's bothering me, then you give me a crappy answer like that?" Harvey crossed his arms. "That's not good enough."

Max nodded. "You're right, kid. You deserve an honest answer." He paused. "Where to start …" Max rubbed his hands on the steering wheel. "I could feel anger toward my former partner Thomas for stealing my case-breaking research on the McFadden assignment ten years ago and taking credit for it, as well as a nice bonus."

"That's cold. No wonder you hate him."

"I said I could be mad at him for that, but that alone would border on petty. It is a good indicator of his low moral fibre though. That's where I really have a problem with Thomas Finkle. He's not honest. Has no integrity. Doesn't believe in rules."

"I thought you had that in common – not following the rules."

Max looked angrily at his partner, his face red. "I may bend the rules from time to time to solve a case, but they exist for a reason. I don't ignore them for my own personal gain."

"What has he done?"

"Selling agency information, taking bribes to make cases go away against certain criminals … you get the idea."

"Wow!" Harvey exclaimed, shifting in his seat. "Why haven't you busted him?"

"Proof, kid. Proof." Max sighed. "I have no proof that will stand up in court, and he knows it."

"That's got to feel frustrating," Harvey replied.

"You've got no idea."

A beep came from the computer.

"Here we go, Max," Harvey proclaimed as the computer signaled receipt of mail. "Our friend Mr. Tucker is retired army, medically discharged. Wounded and honourably discharged. Has experienced some mental trauma resulting from his injury and service." He paused. "How do you know this stuff? It's like you've got a superpower."

"Just keep thinking that, kid," Max smiled. "What else does it say?"

"Mr. Tucker receives regular treatment for paranoia but is deemed completely harmless," he said.

"That's good to know, based on his size," Max added.

"He's filed multiple complaints with the local police towards the house across the street. At first, they investigated but found nothing," Harvey read.

"But then they found ... what?"

"Nothing. Then they stopped responding on the recommendation of his doctor. Seems the police visits only heightened Mr. Tucker's anxiety."

"What about the owner of the place across the street?"

"It's owned by a Mr. B. Justice. Not much information on him, from what came across. He's owned it a couple of years," Harvey answered.

"And before him?"

"A Mr. and Mrs. Rudy Schmaltz. They only owned it for a year. Left in a hurry. Bankrupt and avoiding the bill collector, it looks like."

"Anything else?" Max asked.

"Yes, there's a comment attached to that file from a neighbour."

"Let me guess … Mr. Tucker?"

"No, surprisingly. Mrs. Dubois, his not-so-kind next-door neighbour. Here's the quote on file. 'The Schmaltzes came to me in the middle of the night and asked me to forward their mail. They decided to leave town that night. They'd send a mover for their belongings later. They couldn't take it anymore."

"They couldn't take the bills anymore?"

"No," Harvey replied. "The ghosts."

14 Through the Blue Door

Lauren shouted out to her approaching sister.

"About time, little sis."

"Did you bring your boyfriend to protect you?" Tamika asked her friend's sister.

"This is Benjay Marshall," Sarah said, leaning her bike against the fence, then re-taking his hand into hers.

"Benjay Marshall?" Lauren exclaimed. "For real?"

"You mean the kid that just helped take down that scientist?" Tamika asked.

"The one and only," Sarah beamed, suddenly no longer afraid of the house looming ominously in the background.

"Hi," Benjay waved, not knowing what to do or say to such praise.

"Good call, sis," Lauren said. "And I thought you'd show up with one of your girly girl friends … or not show up at all."

"Like I'd chicken out," Sarah said, winking to Benjay. "You're sure nobody's home?"

71

"Nobody's been home for a long time."

"How do we get in?" Benjay asked. "I assume we don't walk in the front door."

"Around back," Lauren replied. "We'll show you the way. Bring your bike."

The four kids walked to the end of the short brick and iron wall that ran along the front of the property but didn't extend very far down the sides. Darkness filled the space between the houses, making it difficult to see their footing. Benjay struggled with his crutches, not complaining though.

"See the grade entrance at the side? That's the way in. Leave your bike with us. And your cell phone."

"Sure, the blue door." Sarah replied, handing over her phone.

Lauren looked at Benjay, her hand out for his phone.

"I don't have one," he replied.

Lauren's face showed her disbelief.

"He doesn't have one, honest," Sarah told her sister. "I had to call his house line." Sarah exchanged her grip on the handlebar for one on Benjay's hand. "Ready?" she asked him.

Benjay nodded. "I'm not too good with stairs."

"Sarah!" Lauren whispered loudly. "No lights, got it? We'll see from outside." She pointed at her watch, "And you need to stay inside for at least twenty minutes, or you lose the dare."

72

15 Mischief

"I hate to say it," Max said, watching the four youths go around the side of the house, "but it looks like you guessed right about those kids."

Harvey smiled. "What do you suppose they're up to?"

"I've got a hunch. Get on the computer. Look up the house address. Not the police database. Google it."

"Sure, Max." Harvey typed in the address. Scrolling through the results, he muttered. "Hmmm, that's interesting."

"Let me guess," Max interrupted. "Urban legend is ghosts have haunted the house for a long time."

"That's right," Harvey said, puzzled.

"First, all the rumours from the neighbours – that seed got planted somehow. And now the kids. No better dare to young kids than a haunted house."

"Why do you think that's what they're doing?"

"Well, for one," Max replied, "it is much more plausible than the shrink ray idea. Plus, I saw two older kids and two younger ones. Has dare written all over it."

"Are we going in after them?"

"Why?"

"What do you mean, 'why'?" Harvey asked. "It's our job."

"You're wrong. It's not our job. You may have let the neighbours believe you were a police office, but you're not. It's up to the local police to decide if this is worth their time. It's not our job to deal with kids doing a B&E. Now, if there were obvious signs of damage or potential harm to other neighbours, we could step in. Our job is to track that thing and find out what it is. Unless it shows up on our radar again, we're just bystanders."

Max's cell phone rang. A second later, Harvey's cell phone also rang.

"Don't answer it!" Max blurted out.

"What?" Harvey asked.

"That's Gordon. Don't answer it."

"How'd you know?"

Max held up his phone. "Thomas is calling on mine. He's probably trying to get our location."

"He can get our location even if we don't answer."

"Yes, but it will take longer. He'll require someone in the agency to track us. By answering, the phone-to-phone trace that the agency installed will activate."

"I take it you know this from experience," Harvey said.

"A useful trick I've used. By the way, you weren't in the room when Thomas explained what he intends to do if he encounters this thing we're tracking, right?" Max asked.

"No, Captain McAvoy asked us to step out. Remember, you two were acting like toddlers fighting over a toy?"

"It looked that bad, did it?" Max sighed.

Harvey nodded. "I assume he'll capture it like us, for study."

"Not like us. Not at all. We want to tranquilize it to learn about it, study it, try to communicate with it. Thomas intends to torture it, kill it. That's how he plans to study it - dead."

"Gordon doesn't know any of that. I'm sure of it."

"Of course not. Finkle will claim the kill necessary for national security reasons or some such nonsense."

"Why would he want to do that?"

Max held up his right hand, rubbing his thumb and two fingers together. "Money. That's why. This thing will become a gold mine as a research specimen. The agency will ship it out to one of our corporate science partners that will dissect it. Finkle will ensure it goes to a company that he's got an arrangement with. He'll get a lucrative kickback. Likely buy himself another cottage or more cars."

"That's awful," Harvey replied. "Makes me sick to my stomach."

"Let's hope he doesn't corrupt your friend Gordon," Max frowned. "Money can be a powerful influence to do bad things."

16 Into the Darkness

Sarah and Benjay both illuminated their watches to note the time. Benjay led the way down the stairs. Sarah stayed a step behind. Both at the bottom, Benjay tentatively reached for the doorknob and turned the old bronze handle. It wasn't locked. He pushed the door open. He instinctively reached for the light switch. He felt the warmth of Sarah's hand on his arm.

"No lights, remember?"

"I forgot," he replied.

"I can't see anything in here!" Sarah noted.

"Just stand still to let your eyes adjust. That should allow us to see a bit anyway."

"From outside I saw the small basement windows covered up." She squeezed his arm a little tighter. "I don't want to sound cowardly, but can you lead the way?" She hovered close to him.

"I'll try," Benjay said. "I guess I can put one crutch out in front of me to feel our way."

77

He moved forward, whacking Sarah with one of the crutches in the process.

"Ouch!" she cried out. "How about you use one crutch and lean on me? I'll carry the other crutch. That is easier for both of us," Sarah said. "Put your arm around my shoulder."

Benjay removed the left crutch, handing it to her. Steadying himself with the remaining crutch, he put his left arm around her soft shoulder. He inhaled her lightly applied perfume, tingling his senses.

"Thanks," he said, adjusting his weight. "Am I too heavy?"

"No, you're fine."

"Alright. My eyes have adjusted a bit. What about yours?"

"I can see a few feet in front of me, not much more," Sarah replied.

"Same here. Let's walk forward. I'll let you know when the crutch runs into something."

"Okay, let's go."

They moved forward a few feet at a time. It wasn't only dark. It was eerily quiet. Dead silence. They'd moved about ten feet when Benjay felt something ahead.

"Stop," he said. "Let me feel what's in front." He leaned forward, balancing on her. "Laundry tub. Must be a wall behind it. Let's turn right."

They resumed moving forward.

"Ahhhhhhhh!" Sarah screamed. "Something just touched my foot!"

"Stay still. Let me try to look around."

"It's crawling up my leg!!!!" she squealed.

Benjay looked down and swiped his hand at her leg. "Got it!" He lifted his hand, holding the wriggling creature a foot in front of his face. "It's a mouse. See?" He moved it slightly toward her face.

"I see that." Her face scrunched up as she pulled back from it.

"You're not afraid of mice, are you?"

"Only when they crawl on me in the dark," she replied, her face still showing fear. "What are you going to do with it?"

"I guess I'll put it down under the laundry tub."

"Just push it far enough that it doesn't come right back."

Benjay leaned over, gently nudging the little creature along the ground. He hopped back up and reached for Sarah's shoulder.

"Can you wipe your hand off on your pants or something?"

He complied, though he felt nothing really to wipe off. They resumed their slow walk forward. His crutch soon bumped into another object. He tapped the crutch around for a few seconds. "Stairs. Going up to the main floor."

"Thank goodness. Surely, it's not this dark up there."

79

Benjay removed his arm from around her. "I think it's easier to hop up on my own. Do you mind leading, so I know how many steps there are?"

"Do you need the other crutch back?"

"No, I can use one plus the railing. Thanks though. Go ahead. Please count as you go."

Sarah counted aloud until she had reached the door at the top. "Nine," she finished. "I'll wait for you to open the door with me."

Benjay reached the last step, bumping into her as he made his final hop. He began to tilt backwards but she quickly clenched his shirt and pulled him into her arms. They stood there embracing for what seemed a wonderful eternity to Benjay.

"Thanks," he finally gasped.

"You're welcome," she replied, voice cracking. "We should open the door."

"Yes, let's open the door," he replied, pulling back a bit for her to hand him back his other crutch. "I had a thought," Benjay whispered.

"Why are you whispering?" Sarah inquired. "Are you trying to make this place creepier than it already is?"

"Do you think your sister and her friend would dress up like ghosts to try to scare us?"

"You're so smart – I never thought of that!" Sarah replied, slightly above whisper volume. "I wouldn't it put it past them."

"Ready?" Benjay asked, receiving a nod in return. He gingerly grasped the doorknob, which he slowly twisted. He hesitantly pushed the door open. A bone-chilling breeze greeted them.

"Brrrr," said Sarah. "It's a lot colder up here than the basement. That's odd. Isn't heat supposed to rise?"

"A window must be open," Benjay said.

"It still shouldn't feel that much colder. At least we can see better up here." She stepped into the kitchen, looking around for her sister in case she lurked nearby.

Benjay followed. "It looks modern in here. I expected an old, run-down place. You know, falling apart like all those scary movies."

"I don't watch scary movies," Sarah responded.

Benjay laughed. "That's good. This is around the point of the movie where the lunatic comes out of the closet wielding an axe or chainsaw."

"Funny," she replied sarcastically, nudging really close to him.

From behind them both, they felt another cool breeze. They slowly turned their heads to look around. Suddenly, something came hurtling towards them, making a terrifying squawking sound. Grabbing her hand, he pulled her down to the floor as feathers flapped loudly through the space previously occupied by their heads. A large bird made more horrific sounds

81

on its way out the broken kitchen window, knocking the frail curtains off their hooks, the rods clanging into the sink below.

Sarah had landed with a thud on Benjay's chest, her nails digging into each of his arms from fear.

"Thanks, Benjay. You softened my fall!" She remained lying on top of him but loosened her grip. She looked at his red-streaked arms. "I'm soooo sorry." She rolled off him to sit on her knees. "I didn't mean to hurt you."

"I'm okay. It's just a few scratches." He knew better, feeling each fingernail gouge.

"You said you wanted exciting." She looked at her watch. "I hate to break it to you, but we've still got ten minutes."

"That bird's probably the worst of it. We're prepared now in case your sister jumps out at us. Let's check out the rest of the place," Benjay said, sitting up on his knee to reach for his crutches.

"You sure?" Sarah asked. "We could just sit here on the floor for ten minutes. Lauren wouldn't know any better. If she says later that they waited to jump us, we'll just say we didn't go into that room."

"Where's the fun in that?"

"That's the point. I think I've had enough so-called fun for tonight."

"We must at least make it up to the top floor. What do you say?"

82

"Why not." Sarah stood, brushing herself off from the dusty floor. She leaned over to help Benjay off the floor. "I suppose in those scary movies nothing bad *ever* happens on the top floor of a haunted house."

17 Ruckus

Fret had fallen fast asleep in the middle of the dampening field, Shine by his side. Change periodically moved from window to window, checking for signs of danger. To Shine, it already felt like a long time since Faith and Perseverance had headed back to the Globe. Only an hour had passed. It would be a long night.

Shine and Change both jumped at the sound of a screeching bird. The sound seemed to emanate from below them, inside the house. From his knowledge of humans, Change knew very few birds lived in houses. A couple of minutes later they heard human voices. They sounded young to Change. He listened intently to hear their conversation. It sounded like giggling between comments about ghosts.

"I'm going to check it out," Change whispered to Shine. He disappeared through the attic floor. Emerging in the house's upper floor, Change silently glided across the ceiling in invisible mode. Nearing the staircase down, he heard the voices much clearer.

"That's the widest staircase I've ever seen," a boy with a missing leg said.

"Look how shiny the wood is!" the girl said. "This place would be totally cool if it wasn't haunted."

"It's just empty, not haunted," the boy replied. "Big difference. Can I borrow your shoulder again to get up the stairs? There are too many stairs to hop up alone."

The girl moved closer to the boy. He wrapped his arm around her. They slowly moved up the stairs, stopping every few steps to look around.

"Look at the creepy pictures on the wall," she said.

"See the picture of the old woman on the right?" the boy replied.

"I hope it's not her ghost that's haunting this place," the girl said, her shoulders shivering with fright. "She looked scary alive. I'd hate to see her dead!"

"The only ghost we're going to see is your sister with a sheet over her head."

"I hope so," she said as they made it to the landing of the second floor. "There! We made it. Can we go back now?"

"Don't you want to check out any of the rooms?" the boy asked.

"Not really."

Change hoped the kids would turn around. He'd backed up the hallway a bit to stay out of sight, having returned to clear mode. Clear mode came with a small risk of detection, but he could only maintain invisible mode for so long. His morphing capabilities had limited durations too.

"All right," the boy said. He removed his arm from around her. "I can use the railing to hop down."

"I'd rather you kept your arm around me. I don't feel as scared."

The boy wrapped his arm around her again. Suddenly, a crashing sound came from the attic. The girl jumped, then leaned in tightly.

Change slipped through the ceiling to see what caused the ruckus.

"What happened?" Change asked.

"Sorry," whispered Shine. "I didn't notice Fret drifting in his sleep. He knocked over one of the dampening posts."

"The signal went out," Change stated, worried. "Let's hope whoever shot him with that tracker is not nearby."

18 Activated

A single blip appeared on the Detector1000 screen. Then another five seconds later. Then another.

"Where is that coming from?" Max excitedly asked his partner, looking around.

"The haunted place," he replied.

"It's not haunted. Let's call it the Justice place, okay?"

"Fine. I'm recalibrating for proximity." He paused during the machine reset. "Looks like upstairs in the Justice place."

"Great, let's go to the trunk and gear up."

The two hurried to the back of the car. Opening the trunk exposed three duffel bags. Each agent had a bag containing a bullet-proof vest, an extended-range taser, and one of the special modified rifles used at the scientist's house in the dell, in pieces. Assembly of their rifles completed, they grabbed varying rounds of ammo, including trackers and heavy-duty tranquilizers. The third bag contained measuring devices that hung over their necks like long range cameras. The devices measured things like

89

radiation, heat signature, chemical composition, and multiple other elements.

"I've got a feeling we'll get a hit on ectoplasmic energy," Harvey exclaimed.

"We're not ghost busters, Harvey. We need to assess if this thing is dangerous. Then figure out how to capture it. The scientist used electricity. There's no way we can set up an electrified containment field the size of a Victorian mansion. Hopefully, we can tranq it to sleep."

"I'm ready," Harvey stated.

"Really?" Max questioned, smiling at his enthused partner. "Don't you think you should close the trunk with the remaining weapons?"

19 Panic

Shine hovered in the corner, holding the displaced dampening post.

"He slept through the noise?" Change asked Fret.

"Yes, somehow. Can you help me get this pole back in place?"

"Let me do it," he replied, sprouting four arms from his Bubble body. "You can guide Fret back into the centre."

She positioned her boyfriend as requested.

Change held the fallen pole with two arms, failing to align the signal with the other two connecting corners. He stretched one of the other arms to each of those corners to gently nudge them into place. The grid quickly came up, restoring the dampening field.

Shine sighed in relief. "I hope the field wasn't down long enough for humans to detect Fret."

"We'll probably know soon enough," Change replied. "We better get ready to move Fret at a moment's notice."

Shine nodded.

From the corner of the attic they heard creaking wood.

"Get Fret down to the floor right now!" Change whispered loudly to Shine.

Shine complied then looked over at Change for further instructions. What she saw next stunned her. Change's entire body changed to take the shape of an elderly human woman wearing an old-fashioned gown and frilly bonnet. Even his facial appearance changed to pale wrinkled skin with wire-framed spectacles. He held up a human looking hand to his mouth to make a 'hushing' sign against his lips. Change flew straight toward the creaking floorboard.

"Did you hear that?" Benjay exclaimed to Sarah. "The noise in the attic?"

"Yes," she replied, shaking in her shoes. "I vote we ignore it and head down the stairs. Fast."

"Do you think your sister would hide up in the attic? I bet she's trying to lure us up there to scare us. What do you think?"

"If that's what she's trying, she's already succeeded."

"I say we play along and check out the attic."

"You've gotten too brave for me, Benjay. How about I stay here, and you check it out?"

"I might need some help. Let me see." He looked along the ceiling. "There! The door to the attic is near the end of the hall." Benjay left Sarah's side, using his crutches to move directly under the attic door. "I think I can pop it open with a crutch."

"Just be careful," Sarah pleaded.

Benjay leaned against a hallway wall then lifted a crutch up toward the attic door. He flicked the end of the crutch to flip the door release. The door creaked but didn't open. He lowered the crutch to take a breather. Once more, he lifted the crutch. He swung the wooden support at the lever once, twice, three times more. On the third subsequent attempt, the rubber tip of the crutch connected firmly with the latch. The attic ladder came flying down from the ceiling. The old wood of the ladder screamed its resistance to the sudden movement, the noise accompanied by a powerful gust of stale, dusty air. The wooden structure bounced a couple of times on its large overhead hinges before settling into place in a blow of stale dusty air. Benjay jumped back out of the way, staggering on his good leg to stay upright. He unsuccessfully tried to brace himself with the crutch. He fell backwards into Sarah's arms. She had moved forward when she saw him stumbling toward the edge of the ornate staircase. They teetered briefly at the edge but gratefully came to a safe stop at the top of the landing.

Benjay and Sarah separated as they coughed repeatedly, their bodies trying to expel the musty attic exhaust they'd inhaled.

"Ughhh!" Sarah exclaimed, waving at the surrounding air. "That's disgusting! It tastes like a ghost threw up in my mouth."

"Tell me about it!" Benjay gagged.

Sarah fruitlessly wiped at the dust on her clothes. She gave up and looked at Benjay. She broke out in laughter. A fine grey film of dust coated him, bald head to toe. "You look scary!" she giggled.

No sooner had the words come out of her mouth than she heard a couple of eerie 'Ooooo' sounds behind her. She turned to see two very fake looking ghosts at the bottom of the staircase – obviously, her sister and Tamika covered in old bed sheets with eye holes cut out.

Benjay turned to look. As he did, the two wannabe ghosts screamed at the sight of his dust covered ghost-like appearance. At least that's what he thought.

"I guess I ended up scaring them instead," Benjay laughed. "Funny, isn't it, Sarah?"

Sarah didn't reply. The girls at the bottom of the stairs remained frozen in place.

"Sarah?" Benjay turned back to look at her. She had turned completely pale. "Oh, I'm sorry, Sarah. I didn't realize you got covered in dust too." He lifted his hand to wipe her face clean. Except her face wasn't dusty. Her eyes froze in her sockets, looking over his shoulder toward the attic ladder. Benjay slowly turned to look.

Near the bottom of the ladder, in midair, floated the scary old lady from the portrait on the wall. A menacing look emitted from her eyes. Benjay's eyes almost popped out of their sockets.

"Sarah," he whispered. "Slowly back down the stairs."

She didn't budge.

"Take this crutch and hold my arm with your other hand," he encouraged her.

She did, clenching it with newfound herculean strength.

"I'm going to hop back one step. Ready. Go." In unison they descended a step. Then another. Then another. Then another.

The ghost slowly moved from the end of the hall to position itself at the top of the stairs as they neared the bottom.

"Give me my other crutch. Get ready to turn and run," Benjay whispered to Sarah. He looked over his shoulder. Lauren and Tamika remained in the same spot, their feet seemingly nailed to the floor. He looked back toward the ghost. It began to move down the stairs, closing the gap between the young pair.

With both crutches firmly in place, Benjay shouted "Now!"

Sarah turned, bolting down the remaining stairs like a flash. She found her sister's hand under the bed sheet and yanked her toward the door. Tamika snapped out of it at the same time.

Benjay hopped as fast as he could, hoping beyond hope that he didn't fall headfirst in his haste to retreat. He could feel chilly air on his shoulders as his feet hit the second bottom stair.

The three girls stopped a few metres short of the door. It burst wide open, noisily splintering off its frame. The girls screamed and jumped back.

Two men in dark suits burst into the room, large rifles raised in front of their chests.

Tamika screeched at an eardrum busting pitch. Lauren in turn let loose a deafening scream.

The younger agent screamed in response.

His howl astounded the older agent.

Sarah and the two ghostly girls rushed between the startled agents, fleeing into the darkness for safety.

The two men turned to watch the girls flee. Rotating back, they saw Benjay hop down the last stair, secure his crutches in place, and frantically propel himself toward them and the open door behind them. Their jaws dropped at the vision beyond the young boy.

"Is that a ..." Harvey stuttered.

"Well, I'll be ..." muttered Max.

The elderly female ghost flew straight toward them, its arms waving frantically. It effortlessly passed through Benjay, then almost reaching the agents, soared up through the high foyer chandelier. Rattling crazily from side to side, and threatening to crash to the floor, the hundreds of small dangling

96

crystals sounded like shattering glass as they violently slammed together. In an instant, the terrifying ghost disappeared through the roof, leaving the agents frozen in place, mouths hanging open.

20 Time for Us to Fly

Change soared into the attic from outside. Shine watched, amazed. His body transformed midflight from the pale old lady ghost to his normal form.

"We need to go. Now!" Change cried out. "Collapse those two dampening posts. I'll get these two," he signaled to Shine.

With the posts shrunk down, he grabbed the four of them. He hid them in a corner behind a broken wooden chair that had sat undisturbed for many, many years.

"Can you wake Fret?" he asked.

Shine nudged Fret to no avail.

"We've got to go! We can't carry him. They'd catch us before we got a kilometre away. You must try harder to wake him."

Sensing the desperation in Change's voice, Shine formed an arm and small hand. She reared back and let loose a ferocious slap on Fret's face. The sound echoed around the attic.

Fret's eyes popped open. "What did I do?!" He looked around stunned, yet still sleepy.

"Fret," Shine pleaded, wrapping an arm around her boyfriend. "We have to leave this place, okay?"

Fret nodded.

"Good," Change called out from near the opening in the floor. "Through the window."

Shine and Fret moved briefly in that direction. A noise from behind startled them.

Change immediately knew the danger that approached. "Hurry! Two adult humans with rifles are coming up the ladder." Change zipped past them to the window. He instantly extended an arm to push the other two Bubbles rapidly toward and through the window. Penetrating the wall beside them, he glanced back to see the first of the two men aim a rifle. The sound of the rifle shot dimmed briefly as Change emerged outside. A second later, the window shattered. Shine's body lunged forward then began to fall limply toward the ground.

21 Outside

Benjay Marshall slowly walked down the front steps of the old Victorian manor. Mouth agape, eyes frozen wide open, face pale, he mindlessly approached the spot where the three girls excitedly rambled about the experience.

"OMG!" Tamika said, voice squeaking, body shaking. "I have never ... have you ever?" She looked at Lauren.

"Are you kidding? Was that what I think it was?" Lauren flapped her hands excitedly. "Did anybody get that on their phone?"

"I doubt either of you did," Sarah said, still shaking but smiling. "You two were soooo scared!"

"Were not!" they protested loudly together.

"Want to bet?"

"Show us some proof," Lauren said to her sister. "I didn't see you have your phone out filming it."

"You're right," Sarah said. She showed her phone that Lauren had dropped in the excitement. She held it up in front of

101

the girls. "Smile!" she called out as she clicked the button, once facing Tamika and a second time at Lauren.

"How's that going to show we were scared?" Tamika asked, defiantly crossing her arms.

"Look down," Sarah replied, smiling.

The older girls looked down, the front of each of their pants wet. They looked at each other, blushing in embarrassment.

"Give me that phone right now!" demanded Lauren.

"Admit you were scared. I know I was," Sarah told her.

"Alright, I felt scared. More scared than ever before. We saw a real flipping ghost, you know. We all saw it."

"Good," Sarah said. "Now I have you on video too." She waved her phone in front of her.

"You have to get that phone from her, Laur," Tamika pleaded. "We'll get laughed out of school if that hits the socials!"

Sarah laughed. "Chill. Here," she said, tossing her phone to her sister. "Delete them if you want."

Lauren caught the phone and flipped through it to remove the picture and video. She tossed it back, winking at her sister.

"Let's go, Tam," Lauren said. "Don't want other people seeing us like this." She looked at her sister. "Your boyfriend doesn't look very good – you better get him home too."

Sarah looked back at Benjay. His face no longer showed complete fear, but he stood silent.

"Are you okay, Benjay?"

"Oh, yeah," he replied, coughing to clear his throat. "We better go to the backyard to get your bike."

As they began to walk around the side of the house, they heard a gunshot from the other side. Sarah told Benjay to stop and wait, knowing she'd recover her bike quicker without him. Running with her bike, she found Benjay fidgeting nervously, looking at the old house. He secured his crutches, jumped on her handlebars, and she sped away.

"That felt incredible!" she exclaimed. "I'm glad you convinced me to check out the upstairs."

"Weren't you scared?" Benjay asked.

"Never more in my life!" Sarah replied. "My heart's never beat that fast. The carnival's haunted house and roller coasters have nothing on seeing a real live ghost."

He turned to face her. "But it wasn't ..."

"Live? I guess since a ghost is dead it can't be a real live ghost." She laughed at herself.

"No, I mean it wasn't ..." he started to repeat. The bike slowed to a stop. He looked forward again and spotted his street sign. They had returned to the corner near Benjay's house. Sarah held his crutches during his dismount. He placed the crutches under his arms, walking beside her again.

"Stop for a second, Benjay," she whispered to him, standing with her bike between her legs.

"What is it?" Benjay whispered back, moving closer to hear her.

"I wanted to say thank you for going with me. You acted very brave."

Benjay blushed.

Sarah leaned forward, softly kissing him on the lips.

Benjay blushed more.

She hopped back on the bike seat. "What were you saying?"

Benjay couldn't remember, stunned by his first real kiss.

"Benjay?" she asked again.

"What were we talking about?"

"Ghosts. I said how thrilling it felt to see a real live ghost. Well, not live, but you know what I mean."

"Oh, yeah. Ghosts."

"What were you going to say?" she asked as they stopped at the walk leading to Benjay's front door.

"You won't believe me," he stated.

"Try me," Sarah smiled.

"I've had that feeling before."

"Getting scared to death by a ghost?"

"No, the feeling when it flew through me."

"Seriously? The ghost flew right through you? When did that happen?"

"You had just gone outside with your sister and her friend. Those two secret agent types had burst through the door, and you'd run between them. I felt a cold chill up my spine. I knew it hovered right behind me. I froze in fear."

"And then?" Sarah asked.

"Then it flew right through me."

"What did it feel like? Did it hurt? Was it slimy?"

"It kind of tingled like a little jolt of electricity, but it didn't hurt," Benjay replied.

"How creepy," she shuddered. "You survived a ghost attack!" Sarah exclaimed.

"No, I didn't," he stated.

"But you just said the ghost flew through you!"

"No," Benjay replied. "You said a ghost flew through me. I said 'it' flew through me."

"I'm confused," Sarah said.

"Something flew through me, but not a ghost."

"What was it then?"

"A Bubble."

"What's a Bubble?" Sarah inquired.

Benjay looked up at his front window, noticing his mother peeking out from behind the curtain. He looked at his watch.

"You should get home," he told her.

"That's not fair, Benjay Marshall. Leaving me in suspense like this."

"I'll tell you all about the Bubbles some other time, promise," he whispered.

She leaned forward and gave him a second kiss, this time a light peck on the cheek.

"I'm going to hold you to that promise."

22 Knocked Out

Change's heart raced seeing Shine plummet toward the grass below. Sleeping Bubbles float. Unconscious ones don't. They don't bounce either. They land hard, like a human falling from heights. Unsupported by Shine, Fret began to fall too, though much more gradually. Change sprang forth two hands to catch Shine seconds ahead of her striking the ground. He quickly lifted her upward, placing her gently to rest in a fork between two large tree branches. With Shine safe, he swooped back to catch the aimlessly wandering Fret drifting straight into the neighbouring house. Change carried the other half of the young couple to the same tree, nestling Fret against his girlfriend. Change floated into the protective cover of the tree branches, stopping to catch his breath.

"Think quickly, Change," he said quietly to himself. He found a small mark on the surface of Shine's back. Fortunately, it didn't penetrate deeply like a bullet or another tracker. She would recover, provided he could keep her out of human hands. She would be unable to fly on her own for many hours. He looked over at Fret, who'd fallen back to sleep. Change knew he couldn't carry both Shine and Fret. With the tracker still embedded under his skin, Fret posed the immediate risk. The humans who tranquilized Shine would soon arrive. Change lifted Shine, carrying her much higher into the remaining cover of tree branches. Unconscious, she'd retain her normal dark green hue. Hopefully her colouring would provide some advantage by making her less visible from the ground to the human hunters, blending in with the leaves much better than Change's own amethyst skin. Fret's indigo shade would be irrelevant as long as the tracker remained under his skin.

Change bent a few branches to cover Shine, looked at her from a few lower angles to ensure he'd hidden her well, then returned to Fret. Picking up the sleepy and tagged Bubble, Change could hear the humans approaching. He surrounded Fret and went to invisible mode. He hoped to provide sufficient coverage to hide the younger Bubble. Hopefully it would also distort the tracking device. Flying straight up, he heard the men yelling to each other. A rifle sounded several times – the humans couldn't have seen the Bubbles though, as the shots came nowhere near the fleeing flyers.

"Well," Change whispered to his sleeping companion. "I think we have flown high enough for me to go transparent." He stopped surrounding Fret, instead wrapping him in a makeshift arm that looked more like a sling. "We'll have to keep zigzagging till daylight. Then we can head to the alternate rendezvous point to get that tracker out of you. Hopefully, you'll be awake by then – and Shine will stay safe till then."

"Shine … ," Fret mumbled in his sleep.

23 New Trail

Max Killjoy felt he'd nailed that thing with a tranquilizer. Whatever it was. Behind his partner Harvey, he'd hustled down the creaky attic stairs and the handsome wood staircase from the second floor to the large foyer at the front of the house. The fractured front door let in the cooling night air. They'd rounded the side of the house, weapons drawn, expecting to see the thing lying on the ground.

"Where is it?" Harvey yelled, huffing. He leaned on both knees to catch his breath.

"I'm the old guy, remember?" Max hollered back, barely breathing hard.

Harvey straightened up. "Do you see it or not?"

"No," Max replied, his eye fixed on his rifle's zoom as he scanned the area.

Harvey pulled on a pair of night vision goggles. He too combed the surrounding area.

Bang! Bang! Harvey's rifle fired a couple of rounds of tranquilizer darts.

"What are you shooting at?" Max barked at the younger agent, irritated by the surprise shots.

"Thought I saw something move," Harvey replied. "Did you see anything?"

"Nothing," Max said, lowering his rifle. "I know I hit it back in the house. That amount of tranquilizer could have knocked out an adult elephant."

"Where is it?" Harvey asked, removing the night vision gear.

"More importantly," Max asked, "what is it?"

"I've never seen anything like it, even in the department's alien database."

"We have an alien database?" questioned Max.

"Sure, it's required reading in the academy now."

Max shook his head. "They certainly fill your head with lots of crap in the academy these days."

Harvey ignored his partner's comment. "What do you think it is?"

"Don't know. I know I counted three of them."

"Three? I only saw one. Are you sure?"

"Yes, I'm sure," Max answered. "We know they have some ability to cloak their appearance, however I could see their reflections in the window before my bullet shattered it."

"Cloaking, huh? Now you're the one that's gone all sci-fi on me," Harvey laughed.

"That's what the scientist noted in her journals and exactly what I saw. I'm sure my dart hit one of them," Max said, looking around again. He looked up. "What if it didn't make it all the way to the ground?"

"You mean maybe it crash-landed in a tree?"

"It's possible."

"Yeah, I thought of that earlier," Harvey replied. "I even scanned the trees with the night vision goggles. No sign of life."

"As we know it," Max replied. "What about that plasmametre thingy hanging around your neck? Any readings on it?"

"Ectoplasmic radar gun – let me see," Harvey said, flicking on a switch on the side of the device. He slowly rotated in a complete circle. He flicked it off. "Nothing," he replied.

"What about the tracking device? Is it nearby?"

"That's the machine hanging on your neck, Max."

"Oh, yeah," Max grinned. He removed it from his neck, placing it on top of a nearby stump. "Let me see," he scrunched up his face as he played with the buttons.

"You want me to do it?" Harvey asked, reaching toward the device.

"No!" Max exclaimed, swatting at his partner's hand. "I got it." He held up the device. "See – looks like it's moving away, westward."

"Right you are – about a kilometre away already. Should we head back to the car?"

113

"Not just yet. Let's go back upstairs to run some more scans. Maybe one of your contraptions will pick up something useful. Then we'll have to call the local uniforms to board up the front door, if the neighbours haven't called already. We can't leave Mr. Justice's place open like this."

24 Vela Clan

Faith escorted Perseverance back to his home in the Globe, thanking him for all he'd done to help Fret. She went straight home and ate a quick meal, despite a desire to crash her lab to dive straight into research. She didn't think she could sleep with all the thoughts racing through her mind, but fatigue took over.

Waking, but not rested after only a few hours, Faith made a quick stop to inform Justice of the recent events and her intention to visit the Vela clan. Justice agreed to work with Hope to send fresh batteries to Change first thing in the morning.

"I know your friend Cura's resume is unparalleled. If anyone can devise a means to remove this without further harm to Fret, Cura is the one. I've no doubt of that," Justice told Faith.

"It sounds like there is a 'but' to that sentence," Faith replied.

"You know my mannerisms too well, my friend," Justice smiled briefly before his expression turned dour. "We have not exactly been on best of terms with the Velans as of late. The incidents over the past weeks have exacerbated the issue."

"Surely you wouldn't have left Hope and I for human experimentation!" Faith exclaimed.

"The point," Justice said sternly, "is that we allowed our compassion for a single human to jeopardize the entire Bulle clan. Possibly all clans. The Velans are completely justified in their concerns, I'm afraid."

"We had our reasons, you know that. The Velans exaggerate …"

"Do they? What if we didn't free you? What if the entire human race learned of our existence? Learned of our abilities? How long before they deem us a threat and take steps to neutralize, or worse yet, eliminate that threat? We've all seen the horrors that they've inflicted upon the countless species that they've driven into extinction."

"We've saved some species and keep them thriving in the globes," Faith noted.

"Unicorns, Bluebucks, and a few others – a small sample size. Who would save us from such a fate?'

Faith shrugged; she had no answer.

"Exactly. They attack and kill their own kind in large continental size wars, for crying out loud."

Justice sighed a deep breath. He knew no words would stop his friend from her quest, but he had a few more to say.

"You need to exercise caution, my dear friend. Many Velans will not welcome your presence, even for a brief visit. Please do not get into any philosophical debates on human interaction during your visit." He looked straight into her eyes. "Promise me please, Faith."

She nodded acknowledgement. "Promise."

Justice felt he'd done his duty by bringing the issue forward. He reached back to grab a small token from a shelf.

"This will grant you passage into the Vela globe. Just show it – don't let them take it, or even touch it for that matter. It took a long time for us to negotiate this diplomatic pass."

"Understood, Justice."

"Do you need a security officer to go with you? They likely won't be granted passage with the token. They could escort you to the Vela globe and back."

"I think I'll be okay. Thank you for looking out for me." She paused for a minute to fully consider his offer. "You know, maybe I will take you up on the offer. Even if the security officer can't enter the Vela globe, I can do periodic check-ins with them. That way if the Vela decide to not let me leave as scheduled, the security officer can return here to report it."

"Good idea. Just don't get so distracted with your work that you forget to check in. I'd hate to have the security officer sound a false alert."

Faith blushed, knowing full well the validity of Justice's concern.

"I'll have a security officer waiting for you at the portal. Best of luck," Justice finished, a hopeful smile on his face.

25 Late

Peepers had left home with her brother Brawny just ahead of daylight, knowing the Elders counted on them to safely transport the spare batteries to Change. It was a big responsibility. It only came after some serious pleading with her mother that she could accompany her strong older brother.

Brawny's strength made him an easy selection for the Elders. The Elders had a desire to limit the number of trips to haul fresh batteries to aid Fret, then return the depleted batteries for recharging. He could carry the weight of twelve batteries without breaking a sweat. He'd also received training in the setup and calibration of the dampening field. Above all, Brawny had a proven record of responsibility.

His little sister had none of the above qualifications. She could lift a single battery and possibly carry it to the surface – mainly due to gravity doing much of the work. A set of four to re-enable the dampening field was out of the question. Her younger age meant she'd not received any schooling on

119

electronics above the fundamentals, meaning she didn't know a dampening field from a cornfield. And responsibility hadn't wasted much of its time waiting for her to embrace it.

Why did her mother let her go? Persistence? Foolishness?

"Faith," her mother Hope told her.

"You mean you have faith in me?" the girl Bubble grinned.

"I mean the Elder Faith believes in you," her mother responded. "Not that I don't have faith in you my dear. I'm not sure how, but you have a knack for getting out of tough spots. I felt confident that you could do it again. I needed to hear it from someone that I trust. Faith provided that reassurance."

"Thanks, Mom," the girl replied. "I thought I might get grounded for life after that last bit of excitement."

"Oh," her mother said. "Don't think you're off the hook for that little caper. The Elders agreed to temporarily pause your discipline. If you misbehave, your punishment will become double, or worse, I'm afraid. It was a condition of you going."

The girl frowned, face slumping down.

"But don't worry about that for now," her mother smiled. "Besides, I'm sure I can sweet talk them down to something less severe with a good outcome."

"Thanks, Mom" the girl smiled. "Don't worry, you can count on me."

"I am counting on you. So is Fret. Keep those big, beautiful eyes wide open. Brawny may get distracted carrying his heavy load, plus he doesn't get off Globe that much."

"I will, Mom."

"Good luck, Peepers."

26 Resuming the Search

The two agents spent a couple of hours tracking the signal of the thing they pursued.

"Max?" Harvey asked, his gaze fixed on the tracking machine.

"What?"

"We need to come up with a name for this thing."

"Things," Max corrected him.

"That's my point. We can't keep calling them things. We need to name them."

"All right," Max grinned. "How about Larry, Moe, and Curly?"

"Who?" the young agent asked.

"The Three Stooges. Heard of them?"

"My grandpa made me watch them onc time."

"Sheesh," Max complained, suddenly feeling old.

"I didn't mean proper names – I meant we need a word to use for our logbooks. What about 'Blobs'?"

"I picture Blobs as slithering masses that eat everything that gets in their way," Max replied.

"You mean like Lieutenant Slack?"

"Good one, kid," Max laughed. "I think he can eat a dozen donuts without putting a dent in his appetite."

"Then what about Flying Blob?"

"Blobs don't fly, they slither."

"Okay. What about Flubbles?" Harvey suggested.

"Flubbles?"

"Yeah, Flying Bubbles, shortened."

"Flubbles, huh? Are we still talking about Lieutenant Slack?"

Harvey laughed. "I'm open to other suggestions."

"Let's just use Bubbles, okay?"

"Sure, Max. Bubbles it is." Harvey looked at the tracking machine screen. "It's veered hard left."

Max looked left. Nothing but cornfields. He sighed and pulled the car onto the gravel shoulder. "This is a lost cause, kid. I vote we call it a night. Let's go home for a few hours of sleep. In the morning, we can see about requisitioning a chopper to follow these things."

"Not things," Harvey corrected. "Bubbles."

27 Morning

Change hovered sleepily inside a large drainage pipe under a small lightly used gravel county road. Fret lay sleeping on the rocks beside him. Occasionally a truck would rumble overhead, loose stones spraying over both sides of his hideout and perking up the physically tired Bubble. He'd carried Fret around the countryside for over eight hours with only brief rest breaks. With the sun slowly rising, Fret had just begun to show signs of waking from the operating anesthetic. The latest truck completed the job.

"Where are we?" Fret asked groggily, reaching for his sore side.

"In the county, about twenty kilometres from the safe house," Change replied.

Looking around, Fret began to panic. "Where's Shine!"

"She's safe," Change tried to reassure him. "The humans hit her with a tranquilizer. I hid her. I couldn't carry both of you.

125

I checked on her a few hours ago. She continued to sleep peacefully."

"You should have carried her to safety, not me," Fret protested. He moved close to Change to confront him. "Who are you to decide?"

"I'm the one the Elders put in charge, that's who," Change harshly replied, beginning to lose his temper.

Fret moved back.

Change paused for a minute. "Listen, I'm sorry I snapped at you. I haven't slept. I'm exhausted from carrying you all night. Shine's not the one with the tracker stuck in her side. They can't easily find her. You they can. In my judgment, so far, I've kept you both safe. That's what I was tasked to do."

"Of course," Fret said. "I'm sorry to doubt you. It's just …"

"You don't need to explain. I understand how you two feel about each other."

"Thanks," Fret replied, regretting his outburst. "What's our next step?" he inquired.

Change looked at the position of the sun on the horizon. "We can go to the backup rendezvous point now. Someone should have arrived by now to help us. I'm sure Shine will join us when she comes around."

28 Vela Globe

Faith welcomed the company on the trip to the Vela globe. Having gotten to know her companion during the trip, Faith realized why they assigned Tempo. Tempo's flight speed only came second to Jet's, meaning the young security officer could get back to the Bulle globe in half the time it would take the other security officers. Justice obviously saw that need as a realistic possibility.

"Wish me luck," Faith said to Tempo as the pair neared the Vela globe portal.

"See you in two hours," Tempo replied, then remembering Justice's advice added, "and don't forget – I have strict orders to leave promptly if check-in does not occur on schedule."

Faith gulped at the severe tone, the seriousness of the moment suddenly kicking in. "Not a minute longer than two hours," she replied, feigning a smile. She pulled out the token, looked it over, then proceeded to the gate with the token firmly held in front of her. *Don't let them touch it*, she reminded herself as the portal officer ordered her to stop and show identification.

"Hand that over. I need to confirm its authenticity," the officer ordered.

"I will not," Faith replied. "You are young. I trust you have perfect eyesight, or you would not have this important position of ensuring safety of your globe's citizens." She wondered if that last bit sounded a bit too patronizing. She flashed a confident smile.

"Very well," the officer replied. "Flip the token over, please." He looked at Tempo. "Your friend will have to wait out here. The diplomatic token is only good for one entry."

"Understood," Faith said, nodding to Tempo. "Can you please direct me to Dr. Cura's office?"

The officer quickly gave her directions while opening the portal for her to enter.

The Vela globe had many similarities to the Bulle home space, though a few differences were strikingly obvious. The Bulle homes were vibrant with colour, almost looking alive themselves. The Vela housing, and all other buildings for that matter, came in two shades of grey – dull and duller. Faith found the place a tad depressing for its lack of colour and universal sameness. Instead of a gently flowing stream running throughout the globe like in the Bulle home, a much larger river flowed quickly throughout. She should have expected things to be bigger – the Vela globe's circumference nearly doubled that of the Bulle globe.

Following the river's eastern tributary as instructed by the security officer, Faith stopped suddenly, seeing the river rage toward a precipice. Flying past, she couldn't believe the majestic waterfall on the other side. A small rainbow hung across the top, giving the appearance of a gateway for the water barrelling over the edge. She marvelled at the effort it must have taken to create such a spectacle inside a globe. Turning away from the falls, she could see the university directly ahead. She'd seen the thousand-year-old castle-like structure in pictures that in no way did it justice. The architecture almost rivalled the waterfall in its beauty. Perhaps the Vela made their housing look dull to make these monuments more magnificent.

Faith had met Cura at three conferences, none of which occurred at Vela or Bulle, strangely enough. She announced her arrival at the university. The receptionist dispatched someone to retrieve the doctor. Faith had expressed the urgency of the matter. The receptionist favourably received Faith's message.

"Faith, my dear colleague. Good to see you!" Cura sported a large grin.

"It's good of you to see me on such short notice," she replied.

He raised a hand to disperse her concern. "It's the least that I could do. Your presentation at the last conference really struck a chord with me. I've leveraged some of your ideas for my

129

neurology research. It's extremely fascinating what I've started." He paused, putting a hand over his mouth. "My apologies. I get excited talking about my work, but that's not why you came all the way here. Please tell me how I can help."

Faith glanced around. "Is there somewhere private we can talk?"

"Certainly," Cura looked around. "This way," he motioned her to follow. He entered a small conference room, closing the door behind them.

"Thank you," Faith said. "My issue relates to a human interaction. I know many of your leaders firmly oppose any contact."

"I understand your desire for secrecy."

"You may have heard of our recent, um, intervention in human criminal activity."

He smiled. "While I found it fascinating, there were others in Vela that expressed shock and outrage."

"Some of our own Elders hold a similar view of the events. Especially since an Elder and one of our promising graduate students got shot with tracking devices by the humans."

"Really!" The doctor paced, rubbing his chin. "How did you resolve that problem?"

"It's not resolved. That's why I'm here. I had success surgically removing the tracker from the Elder; however, when I began to remove the other device, I found it implanted too close to vital organs. I had to patch Fret back up."

"Is he the one that came with you?"

"No, he's not."

"That's a relief. We wouldn't want the humans tracing him here."

"Nor do we want him coming back to our globe. He's been on the surface trying to avoid detection for days now. At least I hope he's managed to elude them. He's got help but each day heightens the risk of capture."

"I see the dilemma."

"I hope that your advanced surgical equipment and skills can extract the device."

"I'm afraid the equipment you're thinking of will be of no use. It is too large to move to the surface and there is no way you'd ever get Vela approval to bring the young man here." He shuffled around, thinking. "You said you did the initial surgery?"

"Yes, on the surface."

"Do you have images you can show me?"

"No, sorry." Faith could have taken a mini imager to the safe house and captured some images. She hadn't expected that need. An idea came to her. "What about a mental merge?"

Cura looked confused.

"I mean I have the images in my mind. You could merge with me, and I'll share the images."

"Oh," he replied. "Mental merges are frowned upon here, except with couples."

"Back home it's the same," Faith replied. "Privacy violations are a legitimate concern. This is completely consensual and will only take a minute. It will be our secret should you feel you must conceal it from your other Elders."

The doctor looked at her. "I haven't done a mind merge in ages. I'm not sure that I can navigate your thoughts with any precision. I may stumble across things you don't want me to know."

"I will help guide you. I'm not sure we have a choice, short of you going to the surface to examine Fret for yourself."

"That is a good point. Okay, I'll do it. But I'm going to withdraw if I can't get to the image within a minute or so. Deal?"

"Deal. Let's start," Faith said, not wanting to delay further.

The two clan Elders moved close together. During a body merge, two Bubbles join their entire physical forms to make a bigger, stronger entity for lifting or other manual tasks. The brains continue to function independent of each other. During the mind merge, most of their bodies remain separated except one or more of the brain's lobes that interact. Only the occipital lobes in the brain connected, to limit the exchange to images in this kind of mind merge. This would restrict the information available for exchange to the billions of images in Faith's mind, but not the thoughts associated with those images.

Faith felt Cura's presence in her mind. She'd only mind merged a few times, usually with ill patients who she needed to prop up mentally. Experiencing a strong, above average intellect mind inside her mind left her slightly uncomfortable and unsure. She found him wandering through images of her past that she didn't want him to see. She imagined taking his hand. He began to follow her out of the dark caverns of her mind toward the images of Fret's surgery. He studied the images from multiple perspectives then asked Faith to guide him out.

"Wow," Cura exclaimed. "Sorry about the start there. I felt like a child wandering around a dark room trying to find a door out but running into scary monsters at every turn. I'm glad you took my hand."

"I'm sure you'll keep anything else you saw to yourself," she asked.

"Certainly, though I'm not sure I really understood much of it."

"Even better," Faith smiled. "What do you think of Fret's situation?"

He sighed. "I see why you stopped your surgery. You got very close to paralyzing him for life."

"Do you have any ideas?"

"I'm afraid conventional surgery won't help. He's going to have that tracker in his body his entire life."

"Oh, dear!" Faith cried out. "What am I going to tell Hope?"

"This is Hope's boy?" Dr. Cura replied.

"Didn't I say that?"

133

"No."

"Does it make a difference?"

"I might have just written him off otherwise, unfortunately."

"But?"

"But you know the Vela owe Hope a debt. A sizable one at that for her providing our clan with early samples of the Covid vaccine." He thought for a minute. Faith took her turn to pace. "Let's go to my lab," Dr. Cura finally said. "I have an idea!"

29 Gone

Peepers and Brawny arrived at the old house where Faith had unsuccessfully tried to remove Fret's tracking device.

"Something's gone wrong!" Peepers exclaimed. She saw no sign of any of the Bubbles.

Brawny placed the heavy power cells on the attic floor. "Are you sure this is the right place? What happened to the dampeners?"

"I'm sure it's the right place, but good question – where did they put the dampeners?"

The two Bubbles began a search.

"Look," Brawny called from the opposite side of the room. He pointed at the floor. "The door below is open."

"Interesting," Peepers replied. "Why would they open the door?"

"They wouldn't," Brawny replied. "A human must have done it."

"That's not good," Peepers replied. "We'll search the house once we find the dampeners."

"Got them," Brawny called out, holding one above his body.

"Great! Bring them over to the power cells. We'll have to take everything with us."

Brawny stacked the items together, ready for their departure.

"Oh oh!" Peepers called out. "The window is broken." She moved close to glance outside. Nothing looked out of place below, aside from some shards of glass.

"Signs of a skirmish, it looks like," Brawny stated. "Let's check the rest of the house."

Peepers nodded and the two Bubbles flew off, looking for their missing brother, Shine, and Change. The search only took a few minutes, to no avail.

Brawny picked up the power cells and two of the dampening rods. "Can you carry the other two poles?" he asked Peepers.

She lowered herself to the ground and formed arms. Heavy to her, she managed to lift them. For now. She couldn't be certain how long she could carry the poles.

"You lead," Brawny said. "You've visited the alternate rendezvous point previously, not me."

Peepers flew through the broken window, changing her flight path to navigate above a large oak tree. Flying directly above the tree, she called out to Brawny. "Stop!"

"Are they too heavy?" Brawny asked.

"No, look down," Peepers answered.

"What? All I see is a tree."

"Look in the tree – Shine's in the tree."

"What? Why would she be in the tree?"

"Let's go find out," Peepers replied.

The two Bubbles floated through the tree branches to where Change had hidden Shine.

"Do you want me to wake her?" Brawny asked.

"Shhh!," Peepers whispered. "I think I hear something.

"Oh Fretsy Petsy," Shine said quietly in her sleep.

"Gross!" exclaimed Peepers. "Please wake her up before she says anything else I'll regret hearing!"

Brawny nudged the sleeping Bubble. "Wake up, Shine."

"Fretsy?" the groggy girl asked.

"No, it's Fret's brother Brawny."

Shine stretched with a yawn. "Where's Fret?" She looked around as she floated off the branch. "Where am I?"

Peepers approached Shine. "You're near the safe house. We haven't seen Fret or Change."

"Why are you in the tree?" Brawny asked.

Shine closed her eyes, trying to remember. "We had gotten ready to leave the house. We heard humans entering the attic. Change made Fret and I leave first. I thought we'd be safe …"

"But?" Peepers inquired.

"I don't remember," Shine strained to recall the details. "Wait! Something hit me. In the back." She tried looking over her shoulder, spinning around like a dog chasing its tail. "Do you see anything back there, like the tracker that's in Fret?"

"Stay still," Brawny pleaded. He looked at her back. "Peepers! Look at this mark."

The young Bubble looped behind Shine.

"Hmmm," Peepers said. "Do you mind if I touch the area, Shine?"

"Go ahead. Is it a tracker? If so, we need to leave."

"Let me look closer." Peepers used her heightened vision to zoom in as she stretched Shine's skin. "Hmmm," she repeated.

"Is that a good hmmm or a bad hmmm?" Shine asked.

"It's a good hmmm. It looks like they hit you with a tranquilizer of sorts, which is why we found you sleeping. I bet Change put you up here for safekeeping while he and Fret flew away to avoid detection."

"That's a relief," Shine sighed. "Where do you think Fret and Change are?"

"Not sure," Peepers smiled. "But I know where they'll be shortly."

"The alternate rendezvous point," Brawny added.

"How far is the other rendezvous point from here?" Shine queried.

"Last time it took me about twenty minutes from here," Peepers responded.

"That's good that you know the way," Shine replied. "Is it another house like this one?"

"It's another house," Brawny said.

"But it's nothing like this house," Peepers grinned.

"Why's that?" Shine asked.

"It's got people living in it," Peepers added.

"Isn't that dangerous?" Worry lines appeared above Shine's eyes.

"Not these people," Peepers laughed. "We're going to the house of Benjay Marshall."

30 Chopper

Max hated paperwork. His recently retired former partner had almost always made Max do the paperwork after cases. Seniority stunk. At least then it did. Now that he had a younger partner, the tables had turned. Max enjoyed spending his time working case clues, preferring Harvey to deal with the mundane administrative tasks. That meant requisitioning a helicopter for this morning's continued search of the Bubble things. The other advantage of Harvey requesting the chopper? Max had worn out his welcome with that department. On a prior assignment, he'd stated the mayor's life was in mortal danger to expedite his helicopter request. In fact, his request had nothing to do with the mayor. The criminal Max pursued just happened to be downtown where the mayor had the job of Grand Marshall for the holiday parade. Max knew the street closures would prevent him from getting to his bad guy before he disappeared into the crowds. A helicopter didn't have such restrictions. At least once he convinced the pilot to ignore the 'no fly zone' over the parade.

"Noon, Max," Harvey stated, hanging up his phone, seated at his desk.

"Nothing sooner?"

"No, sorry. I had to beg to get it that early." Harvey paused. "It is Sunday, you know." He tossed his phone on the desk. "Should I have dropped your name?"

"No!" Max exclaimed, sitting up straight. "I mean, they don't like me down there for some reason." Max closed the case file, done examining the contents. "Can you fire up the Detector1000 to see where our friends have travelled all night?"

"Sure thing," Harvey replied. "Let's go to the meeting room. I can project it on the wall."

"You can do that?" Max asked, before answering himself. "Let me guess … Chapter 13 of the manual?"

"Chapter 12," Harvey grinned, carting the electronic device to the meeting room. In a few seconds he had the path of the Bubbles up on the whiteboard.

"Interesting," Max commented.

"It is cool that I can blow this up nice and large, isn't it?" Harvey replied.

"I'm not referring to that. I mean the pattern. Look at yesterday."

"I didn't see any pattern yesterday," Harvey noted.

"Exactly! Now look at today."

Harvey walked up to the whiteboard. The pattern weaved back and forth, with a narrowing range. The trail formed a funnel shape.

Max grabbed a marker. "Let's see where it would end. Continue narrowing the weave." He drew angling lines that intersected at a point at the end. "Now, assuming that my lines aren't perfectly precise, we could approximate this general area." Max drew a circle around the intersection point. It covered an area of a few blocks.

"That narrows the search area. We could possibly get there ahead of the Bubbles."

Max bent down to view the street names. "There's something about this area that sounds familiar …"

"Can't say I know it," Harvey commented.

"Not sure I do either, but the street names … just a sec," Max said, plopping the marker on the holder in front of the whiteboard. He briskly walked back to his desk.

Harvey watched Max rifle through files on his desk. Finally Max triumphantly held up an orange file folder and paraded back to the meeting room.

"I did recognize those streets. Look!" Max proclaimed, opening the file to hand it to the younger agent.

"You've got a great memory for an old guy," Harvey teased his partner, looking at the included map.

"I've got a mind like a steel trap," Max smiled. "Problem is the old trap's getting a lot of rust."

143

Harvey flipped through other photos in the orange file folder. "What's the name on this file?"

"Marshall," Max replied. He pulled a photo out of the folder. "Here's a picture of the kid, Benjay Marshall. Recognize him?"

"He's the kid from the ghost house!"

31 Lab Tests

Cura led Faith into his laboratory. She expected to see test tubes, beakers, microscopes, and other paraphernalia like her lab. Instead, his lab looked like nothing in the Bulle science building. Electronic devices and wires ran everywhere. The Bulle had limited need for electricity, especially for individual use. To them it was a human concern. The Bubbles noted that mankind's constant quest for more energy often led to war. The earth's resources and environment always suffered at the expense of war.

"What type of research do you perform here? Based on your last research paper, I thought you continued to study stimulation of damaged nervous systems."

Cura sighed. "See that small desk in the corner?"

Faith nodded.

"That is the portion of this lab allowed for such research. Most of my lab, and resources, were, how shall I say it?

145

Redirected. Redirected by the Vela Science Ministry. Ninety percent of my time now is dedicated to their mandated research."

"What could they possibly think is so important?" Faith asked.

Cura blushed. "You're not going to like it."

"I had that feeling seeing the wires."

"The Vela Elders have me developing Destabilizers."

"Sounds ominous. What are Destabilizers used for?

"To disrupt the normal function of the nervous system," the doctor replied.

"To what end?" Faith asked. "What would you accomplish disrupting a Bubble like that?"

"It's not for Bubbles. It's for humans."

"Oh my …," Faith said, her voice trailing off as she contemplated the implications.

"The Destabilizers are for defence purposes only," Cura replied in defence of his actions.

"Don't they always say that?" Faith looked up to the ceiling. "This is not good."

"On the contrary," Cura stated. "A Destabilizer may be just what Fret requires. The voltage emitted should be sufficient to render the tracking device inert, without hurting the boy."

"How do you know it won't harm Fret?" She looked at the doctor, who sheepishly looked at the ground. "You mean you tested these on your own Bubbles?"

"Volunteers only."

Faith frowned. "I'm disappointed, Cura."

"I understand."

"What is it intended to do to humans?"

"Destabilize their nervous system, essentially paralyzing them for a few hours."

"Sounds painful."

"It likely will be."

Faith looked down for a few seconds before turning her gaze back to Cura. "You know this is a waste of your talents, don't you?"

He nodded.

"When this is over, would you have any interest in transferring your other work to the Bulle lab? I'm sure that I can arrange a research position."

"That's very kind, but I don't know that they'll let me go."

"Let you go where?" A rather large Bubble entered the lab.

"Minister Cage!" a surprised Cura called out, louder than he intended.

"Cura," the minister said, "you haven't introduced me to your friend."

"My apologies. This is Faith from the Bulle globe. She needs assistance with a clan member trapped on the surface with a human tracking device in him."

147

"And just how is this a Vela concern? You know our off-globe policies are extremely strict."

"I plan to use a Destabilizer to disable the device. It would be a great live test."

The minister thought about the proposal.

Faith looked at Cura, understanding why the doctor had switched the subject away from him moving his research to the Bulle globe. She felt Cura's request a long shot at best.

"Permission granted," the minister replied.

"Thank you," Cura replied, grinning.

"Of course," Cage added, "there are conditions attached."

"Such as?" Cura asked.

"You will take two senior guards with you, both wearing Destabilizers in case of human intervention." Cage looked at Cura. "That's not a problem, is it?"

"No, not at all," Cura replied. "It will make me feel safer going to the surface."

"Agreed. When do you plan to leave?"

Cura looked at Faith, who replied, "Can you have the guards ready in twenty minutes?"

Cage nodded. "Nice to meet you, Faith. Best of luck with your mission."

"You as well," she responded.

Cage started to leave the room. He turned back to face Cura. "A word in private, please."

The two Velans moved out of the room.

"Cura, I need you completely clear on this assignment. Retrieving the Bulle member is secondary to testing our weapons on the humans. Is that understood?"

"I'd rather not use force," Cura replied.

"Do you want to go?" Cage glared back.

"Yes," sighed Cura. "The priorities are understood."

"Good. The council have expressed extreme concern about the Bulle clan actions recently. There are strong reasons why we deter human interaction. It is quite possible there will be consequences for the Bulle clan after this mission. You want to make sure you are on the right side of that dispute. Testing the weapons will ensure that."

Cura nodded uncomfortably.

Cage departed, feeling confident he'd firmly made his point.

Cura re-entered the room where they'd left Faith.

"He's creepy," Faith whispered, a look of disgust on her face, even without knowing the content of their private conversation.

Cura exhaled. "Now you see what I have to deal with every day."

"I don't trust him," Faith replied.

"You shouldn't," Cura acknowledged. "I certainly don't."

32 Rise and Shine

Benjay awoke well rested. The excitement the night before had tired him out more than expected. He almost always awoke at seven-thirty on Sundays. Today he rolled over to spot eight thirty-six on the red letters of his alarm clock. He momentarily wondered why his mouth tasted awful. Then he recalled that he'd skipped washing his face and brushing his teeth last night. He didn't want to scrub away Sarah's kiss. His first kiss. He felt different today. Better different.

He arranged to walk to church with Sarah. She wanted to hear all about the Bubbles. Benjay just hoped she didn't think he'd gone crazy. He didn't want to scare her off. He liked her. He liked her a lot.

Eating his morning cereal, Benjay heard his sister coming down the stairs.

"How'd the big date go last night? You slipped into bed before I got home from my girlfriend's house."

"It wasn't a date."

"Okay, how'd your un-date go last night?" She smiled, grabbing an empty bowl.

"She's nice. We had fun."

"Cool. My girlfriend and I had fun at the carnival. The rides seem better this year than last. The house of horrors is wickedly scary, but nothing compared to what you did last night." She looked at her brother for a reaction.

"What?" Benjay responded, startled.

"Weren't you scared?" Lindsay asked.

He leaned forward, whispering. "How'd you know?"

"Don't worry, I won't tell Mom and Dad." Lindsay filled her bowl with cereal, followed by enough milk to make the cereal float.

"Thanks," Benjay replied. "But how did you know?"

Lindsay set her cereal down. She pulled out her phone, touched a few buttons, handing it to Benjay. "I guess I was wrong about Lauren. She's not that concerned about looking cool."

Benjay looked at the phone. The screen showed side by side pictures of Lauren and Tamika, the front of their pants wet from peeing them at the sight of the ghost. Under it read a caption. 'OMG - How cool girls react to seeing a ghost!'

"I thought she deleted those from Sarah's phone," Benjay replied with a large grin.

"Sarah took them? Awesome."

152

"Yeah, but Lauren demanded Sarah hand over the phone to delete the pictures. We thought she did."

"Well, she fooled you all. Any girl that will make fun of herself like that is cool in my books."

"Guess so. Glad she didn't include any pictures of me," he paused. "Did she?"

"No, she didn't." Lindsay replied. "My girlfriend took a picture of me screaming at the house of horrors. She tried sending it to me from there, but they have some weird blocker that prevents cell phones from getting a signal. I think they want to discourage live streaming from inside and revealing their tricks. I'll show you the photo when she sends it to me. You'll get a good laugh."

"Thanks, Linds."

"Did you guys really see a ghost?"

"Sort of."

"What do you mean, sort of? You either saw one or you didn't."

"They thought they saw a ghost. They actually saw a Bubble."

"You sure?"

"Absolutely. Once you've had a Bubble fly through you, you remember the feeling."

"Was it anyone we knew? The Bubble, that is."

153

"No, it wasn't like any Bubble I've seen. It looked like a real ghost. Very creepy and dead looking," he shivered his shoulders. "I don't want to run into that again."

"Just as well they thought they saw a ghost. Your girlfriend would think you're crazy if you started talking about Bubbles." Lindsay put a spoonful of cereal in her mouth and looked at Benjay, who suddenly looked down at his feet. "Oh, no, you didn't!" she exclaimed, spitting out bits of cereal before covering her mouth.

"I just told Sarah – not her sister or Tamika," Benjay replied, embarrassed.

"Maybe she'll forget all about it by the time you see her at school on Monday," Lindsay said.

"We're walking to church today. She wants to hear all about the Bubbles."

"That's a big secret to tell anyone. Are you sure you want to do that?"

"Why not?"

"If she believes you, she'll want you to prove it. Can you summon a Bubble to appear to entertain your girlfriend, or even as proof?"

"No," Benjay quietly said, head down.

"So, she won't believe you. Likely just as well," Lindsay stated, standing to rinse out her cereal bowl.

"Why's that?"

"You wouldn't want to make your other girlfriend jealous, would you?" Lindsay asked him.

"What other girlfriend?"

Lindsay grinned and rubbed his bald head, followed by a louder than it felt smack on the top. "Why, Peepers, of course!"

33 Closing In

Max and Harvey pulled up in front of the Marshall residence, surprised to see another black agency vehicle already staking out the place.

"Thomas!" shouted Max. "You didn't tip them off, did you?" He looked at his partner. "No, of course you didn't – sorry I even suggested it."

"They've got to be here on a hunch," Harvey replied. "They don't have the Detector1000 data like we have. It's not linked into the network for them to access."

"I'll tell you one thing," Max grinned. "Gordon must have figured it out because Thomas couldn't find his face in the mirror."

"So, what do we do now?" Harvey asked.

"Let's go talk to them. He'll hate that on a stakeout," Max laughed. "Just follow my lead."

They exited their vehicle to approach the driver's side door of Finkle's car. Max tapped on the driver's side window, though he knew Thomas had watched him approach in the rear-view mirror.

Lowering the window halfway, Finkle turned his head. "Do you need directions, Killjoy? Cause I'd be happy to tell you where to go." Thomas smirked at Max. He turned to laugh toward his partner.

"No, we're good. Thanks though," Max coolly replied, ignoring Thomas's implied insult. "The Kid here and I have come up empty. He tracked you down in case you had any good information that you could share before you go off shift in a couple of hours."

"Nah," replied Finkle. "Gordo here suggested we stake out the Marshall residence, since they had involvement in the original case. Pretty boring so far."

All four agents turned at the sound of a garage door opening at the Marshall house.

"I guess you'll be wanting to follow them. Harv and I will leave you to it. We'll head back to the office. Call us in should you need any backup, okay?"

"Sure thing, Max." Thomas put up his window.

Max could hear Thomas tell Gordon, "That'll be the day" as he started the car. Max strolled back to the car, knowing Thomas eyed him in his rearview mirror.

"Don't look at the house," Max ordered Harvey. "Look forward and walk to the car."

Both men got into their agency vehicle. Max looked ahead to see Thomas's car turn right tailing the Marshall vehicle as it moved out of view. He opened the door and got out again.

Harvey followed. "Aren't we going back to the office?"

Max stared at Harvey. "Really? I said that just to get rid of Finkle. If he knew we'd come here on purpose and planned to stick around, he'd never have followed the Marshall family. I mean most of the Marshall family."

"What do you mean?"

"The boy – Benjay – he wasn't in the car."

"You think he's still home?"

"Not likely. He's too young to stay home alone. But it may mean that he'll come back separately."

Harvey glanced at his watch. "They've likely gone to church. Maybe Benjay went with a friend."

34 Empty House

Approaching from the west, Peepers led the way for Brawny and Shine. She could tell Brawny's arms grew tired from the weight of the load he carried, though he'd never admit it. Assuring the others that she'd regained her strength, Shine lightened Brawny's load slightly.

"Hold up right here," Peepers told her companions as they neared the window of Benjay's room. "Let me go inside to make sure the coast is clear. It will only take a minute."

Peepers slipped through the window into Benjay's room. The room had changed since her last visit. A new colour covered the wall, more of which could be seen now due to less posters. The biggest change was the absence of Benjay. She left his room to search the remainder of the house. She couldn't find Benjay, or any of the Marshall clan. She rejoined the others outside.

"C'mon," she waved. "Let's set up inside Benjay's room.

Brawny's fatigue became obvious as he dropped three of the dampening posts upon entering the house. Shine and Brawny gawked at the contents of the room, having never seen the inside of a human home. They'd both heard stories from Peepers, Jet, and Fret. Seeing it for real felt very different.

Peepers began setting up the dampening poles, letting the others take in the new sights and sounds. With all four posts set up, but not aligned, she beckoned Brawny for help.

"I'll swap in some of the new power cells," Brawny said, moving toward the nearest pole.

Within a few minutes, they'd established the dampening field, flooding Shine with relief. "Hopefully, this will keep Fret safe until Faith can come back to remove that thing completely."

"Let's hope so," Peepers replied. "Since nobody's home, do you want a tour? Benjay explained some of the gadgets they have, though I don't know that I can make them work."

"Like what?" Brawny asked.

"Television, for one," Peepers replied. "It shows images of humans doing stuff. Some of it's real and some of it is pretend. I have no idea how they tell it apart."

"Why would they want to show pretend stuff?" Shine asked.

"I guess it's supposed to entertain them," Peepers answered. "Benjay says it helps elders take their mind off their daily stress."

"Daily stress?" Brawny questioned. "All they do all day is drive around in those cars of theirs."

"There are a lot of cars on the roads. Maybe it's stressful driving around," Shine supposed. "What other gadgets do they have?"

"They have a refrigerator. It keeps their food cold."

"Why?" Brawny asked.

"It keeps the food fresh," Peepers said.

"Why don't they just get fresh food every day?" Shine asked.

"They don't have time, apparently," Peepers stated.

"I guess they're too busy driving their cars around all day," Brawny said.

"That must be where they went today," Shine added.

"Maybe. Only one of the cars is in the ...," Peepers searched for the word. "The gurage. They keep the cars in the gurage. One is missing."

"Doesn't matter, I guess. Main thing is they aren't home," Shine said. "Let's explore!"

Though tired, Change felt invigorated, no longer required to carry Fret. The tagged Bubble unsuccessfully tried to convince Change to change his mind to go back for Shine. Change held firm.

"Can we stop weaving?" Fret asked Change.

163

Change called over to Fret, "Sure, it's only a couple kilometres due west from here. Hopefully the reinforcements have arrived ahead of us and set up the dampening field."

"I know I've slept a lot recently," Fret replied, "but I'm still tired. I could use a rest."

"Ditto on the rest idea," Change sighed. "You've come here before – which house is it?"

Fret pointed. "Let's enter through the upper floor. The machine-boy Benjay lives up there."

"Is he scary?"

Fret chuckled. "Quite the opposite. He's the nicest boy you'll ever meet. It's almost like he's a Bubble."

Change's face expressed relief. "You know that he'll be the first human that I meet. At least without trying to scare them away."

"I guessed. Not many of us have had encounters." He rubbed his side. "And now you know why. Not all of them are like Benjay Marshall."

35 Returning

Church service let out a few minutes early, to the relief of all the parents with restless children. Benjay and Sarah had sat with his parents, although hers also attended the service. Stepping outside, Benjay was surprised to see Sarah's parents greet his parents with an air of familiarity. He didn't realize they knew each other at all, let alone well. Sarah seemed equally surprised.

"We're heading into the bazaar in the community centre with the Lightfoots," Benjay's mother informed him.

"Do you mind if Sarah and I head back to our house?" he asked his mother.

"I'm sorry, honey. You aren't old enough to stay home alone," she replied.

"I'll go with them," piped up Lindsay from behind.

Mrs. Marshall looked at her two children, then over at her husband and the Lightfoots. They all nodded.

"Okay, but same rules as after school – got it?"

"Yes, Mom," Lindsay and Benjay replied.

The four adults moved toward the community centre, quickly into conversation.

"Thanks, Linds," Benjay smiled at his sister.

"Trust me, I didn't do it for you. I didn't want to drag about that bazaar any more than you did. You just gave me a good excuse to get back two hours of my life."

"Thank you anyway," Sarah smiled as she and Benjay followed Lindsay.

Walking around the front of the church, Lindsay hesitated briefly, almost causing Benjay to walk into her.

"What's wrong, Lindsay?" he said.

"Just keep walking," his sister replied.

"What is it?" Benjay asked quietly as they walked on.

"Just wait a couple of minutes, until we get around the corner up here," she said.

Rounding the corner, Lindsay stepped behind a large oak tree. Sarah and Benjay followed suit.

"Did you see that black car in front of the church with the two men sitting in it?"

"No," Sarah and Benjay replied in unison.

"Well, I swear they followed us from home to the church. Mom and Dad didn't notice, but I did."

Benjay laughed. "I think you watch too many spy movies."

"That may be true, but I know what I saw. Those two guys have government agents written all over them."

"So, what are you going to do?" Sarah said, belief filling her voice.

"We're going to go home. I'll call Mom from there. I don't think they're following us. They must be watching Mom and Dad."

"Why?" Benjay asked.

"If I had to guess, I'd say it has to do with your Bubble friends."

"I *knew* they were real!" Sarah exclaimed.

"Do you think they're trying to catch one, like that crazy Dr. Kane?"

"Most likely. I'm sure they'd love to get their hands on a Bubble to study it, like Dr. Kane did."

"That's sad," Sarah said. "Why would anyone want to hurt a Bubble?"

"Some people fear what they don't understand, especially government types apparently," Lindsay sighed.

"Bubbles are scared of people, but they'd never harm us or want to take us apart to study us," Benjay said.

"They sound so nice," Sarah replied. "I hope I get to meet one someday."

167

36 Welcome Home

Carefully watching for pursuit from the government agent types, the three youngsters came to the turn onto the Marshalls' street. Lindsay had Benjay and Sarah wait down the street, near the corner. She used the tall hedge at the corner to creep up to peek at the front of her house. Lindsay returned to the others.

"There's a black car just like the one at the church parked in front of our house. I think we should sneak around to the back door to get in."

Benjay and Sarah nodded. One by one they crossed the street, headed for the street behind their house. They seemed to go undetected by the suits in the car. Fortunately, the Johnsons that lived behind them had grown accustomed to the kids cutting through their backyard. They'd even installed a gate between the two properties. The Johnson kids cut through the Marshall property to the bus stop. The three kids quietly used the gate to enter their backyard and approach the back door.

"Stop!" Lindsay quietly called to the others. "Do you see that?"

"The kitchen lights are flashing on and off!" Benjay whispered back.

"Did your parents get home already?" Sarah asked.

"No, they'll stay at least an hour at that bazaar. Likely longer," Lindsay replied.

"Maybe it's the spies whose car is out front," Benjay offered.

"You guys press up against the wall, out of sight. I'll sneak up and peek."

Sarah and Benjay complied as Lindsay crept toward the window. She slowly raised her head up over the window ledge. What she saw inside surprised her, making her laugh aloud. She doubled over and covered her mouth. She motioned for Benjay and Sarah to come over.

"Take a look!"

Inside, three Bubbles moved around the kitchen checking out everything. A Bubble larger than Peepers opened and closed the fridge door repeatedly to watch the light go on and off. Finally, it went inside and pulled the door closed behind it. Quickly the fridge door flung open, the panicked Bubble flying out, followed closely by a carton of milk splashing to the floor. Apparently, the darkness inside startled the Bubble. It immediately turned to check out the spilled milk.

170

A second Bubble, about the same size as Peepers, hovered near the overhead light. Peepers rapidly flicked the light switch on and off. It looked like the other Bubble attempted to catch the light as it left the bulb. Peepers accidently hit the switch beside the light, turning on the attached fan and sending the other Bubble hurtling across the room, crashing into the cupboards. Peepers laughed so hard that she cried. Seeing the spilled milk, she found a dishcloth to wipe it up. Frustrated at the cloth's dismal effectiveness, Peepers lowered herself to the floor. She absorbed the liquid like a sponge. She flew to the sink and discharged the milk.

"Wow!" Sarah exclaimed. "They're amazing, Benjay."

Peepers looked up, apparently hearing Benjay's name. She streaked toward the window to look out. Upon seeing the three youths outside, she nudged part of her face through the glass.

"Benjay! Good to see you. Quick – come inside."

Lindsay pulled the key out of her pocket. She quietly edged open the back door and entered.

"It's so good to see you, Benjay!" Peepers formed two arms to hug her human friend.

Benjay blushed in front of Sarah.

"Lindsay! Good to see you too," Peepers said, moving her hug to Benjay's sister.

Peepers pulled back to look at Sarah. "Who's your friend, Lindsay?"

171

"I'm Sarah," she said, holding her hand out to shake. "Benjay's girlfriend."

Benjay blushed some more.

Peepers looked at Benjay, then back at Sarah. She looked at Sarah's outstretched hand, uncertain what to do.

"It's called a handshake," Lindsay stated. "It's for people that don't know each other well enough to hug."

"Oh," Peepers said. "How much time must pass before we know each other well enough?"

"It's not completely a matter of time," Lindsay answered. "It's more about comfort around somebody."

"Oh, I see," said Peepers, deep in thought. "Are you comfortable with Sarah?"

"Yes," replied Lindsay.

"Then I'm comfortable!" Peepers exclaimed, grinning. She pushed aside Sarah's still outstretched hand to give her a big hug.

Benjay laughed, seeing the startled but thrilled look in Sarah's eyes.

"I'm sorry," Peepers said, backing up, "where are my manners. Speaking of girlfriends," she motioned to the Bubble on her right, "This is Shine – Fret's girlfriend."

"Nice to meet you," Shine replied, doing a little curtsey-like bob.

"And this big fella over here is one of my brothers, Brawny."

172

Brawny nodded hello, his eyes large with amazement as he looked over the humans in front of him.

"What are you doing here?" Lindsay asked.

"We're waiting for Fret," Shine replied. "He got shot with some kind of tracking device. This is our rendezvous place."

"Why here?" Benjay asked.

"The original safe house has been compromised. This is our backup plan," Peepers replied.

"I don't think it's safe here either," Lindsay said. "There are federal agents or something like that out front in a black sedan. They must have tracked you here."

"I don't think so," corrected Peepers. "I think they figured it worth watching your home, knowing your family's involvement in catching that scientist lady."

"Either way," Lindsay stated, "you can't stay here. It's just a matter of time before they come in here looking for you."

"Maybe, but we have to wait for Fret," Shine pleaded. "He'll get here any minute, I know it."

"As soon as Fret arrives, we'll have to leave," Peepers stated, looking at Shine. "The dampening devices won't do any good if they already know he's here." She looked at Lindsay. "Do you know a safe place?"

"You say Fret has a tracking device?"

The three Bubbles nodded.

"Benjay," Lindsay began to ask, "do you think the tracking device might work like the GPS in my phone?"

"Probably," he answered.

"Definitely," replied Sarah. "My father's into that stuff. He's bored us with many dinnertime discussions about GPS, RF transmitters, and other high-tech gadgets. If he weren't such a klutz, I'd think he was a spy."

"Then I know a good place to hide."

"We just need Fret to show up," Shine said, forcing a smile.

37 Fret Arrives

Change and Fret cautiously approached the Marshall house. Change recommended they do a 'fly by' to check out the place for suspicious activity. A young boy walked a dog down the street. The dog stopped at every tree to leave its scent, beginning to aggravate the boy for its lack of walking on their walk. A dark car sat in front of the Marshall house, with two men inside. A lady pushed a baby stroller down the sidewalk opposite Benjay's home. To the two Bubbles, nothing looked suspicious.

"Let's go in," Change called over to Fret. "You know where to enter?"

"Second floor window on the side," Fret pointed.

Outside the window, Fret looked in. "Nobody's here," he said, disappointed. "I thought for sure they'd have arrived by now."

"Well, I can't stay invisible forever. We better go inside," Change replied.

Moving through the window, the bedroom door burst open. A laughing Benjay and Lindsay entered, followed by another girl. A few seconds later, Peepers, Shine, and Brawny came through the door.

Change and Fret made themselves visible.

"Fret!" Shine called out, rushing to hug her boyfriend.

"Where's Faith?" Fret asked, looking around.

"It's a long story, brother," Peepers replied. "We're going to have to keep you under wraps for a while longer."

"I see you have the dampeners set up. How long will the batteries last?"

"A day, but it won't matter," Brawny replied to his older sibling.

"Why not?" Fret asked.

"The humans already know you're here," Shine told him. "But Lindsay here has a plan to keep you safe."

Fret looked at the teenage girl, waiting for an explanation.

"Can three of you carry those dampener thingys?"

"How far? I'm still a little weak," Fret said, concerned.

"You can't be one of them – you must sit in the middle. I'm afraid Shine or Peepers will have to carry one of them."

"How far did you say?" Shine asked.

"A couple of kilometres."

"Yeah, I think so," Shine smiled. "If I get tired, Peepers could carry it for a bit. Right, Peepers?"

"You bet!" Peepers exclaimed.

"Good," Lindsay said, then continued to explain her plan to the group. Finishing, she heard a loud knock at the front door.

"We better get going right away!" Lindsay exclaimed. "They knocked but I don't think they'll wait for a reply to come in."

The group scampered downstairs, stopping in the kitchen for Benjay and Sarah to load snacks into a small drawstring bag he could throw over his shoulder. Lindsay texted a note to her parents. The kids scanned the backyard for signs of waiting trouble. They saw none. Lindsay placed her tattered favourite pink cap on her head.

"Let's go," Lindsay whispered, grabbing Benjay's baseball cap off the hook by the door and plopping it on his bald head. She held open the door for the Bubbles to pass through in formation, Fret in the middle surrounded by dampeners.

After everyone cleared the doorway threshold, Lindsay quietly closed the door and locked it. Pulling out the key, she heard the front door open.

"Run!" she quietly called out to the others.

Sarah had ridden her bike to the Marshalls' prior to church. She flipped back the kickstand and ran with it. The group quickly passed through the back gate into the neighbour's yard, Lindsay again quietly closing the gate behind them to avoid an obvious trail of a swinging or open gate.

The group headed down the street behind the Marshall house. Benjay called out.

"Lindsay – look! Mom and Dad are getting home." Between the houses they could see their parents' car slowly approaching their driveway.

"Don't worry," she said, patting his bald head. "They'll be okay. They don't know anything so they can't say anything." A smile crossed her face. "Besides, knowing Mom, she's already spotted that black sedan and is calling Uncle Mark at the police station."

Sarah reached for Benjay's hand to comfort him.

Benjay smiled, unsure if Lindsay's explanation or Sarah's touch had put him at ease.

38 Nothing, Yet

Inside the Marshall residence, Max and Harvey quickly concluded that whatever, and whoever, was there, had gone.

"We know it was here," said the frustrated senior agent. "We saw the tracker stop here. What's it showing now?"

Harvey looked at the machine. "It hasn't moved. It should be in the house."

"Maybe the Detector1000 needs recalibrating, again. What time is it, anyway?" Max asked.

"Almost noon," Harvey replied.

"You better get out to the radio. Our chopper's arriving soon."

"What are we going to tell them?" Harvey asked. "We've got nothing."

"Yet," Max said, hand shaking a finger in the air. "We've got nothing yet. Let me check the back for signs of movement." He pointed to the tracker. "And recalibrate that thing, just in case."

179

Harvey left through the front door; Max exited the back. Nothing looked amiss in the kitchen. The back door remained locked. Stepping outside, Max paused to look around. He leaned in close to the kitchen window – fresh fingerprints – someone had recently looked inside. Straightening up, he glanced around the yard. The fence had a gate to the neighbour behind. Two trails led from the gate – one directly to the door where he stood and a second alongside the house. One trail for the neighbours to cut through and another for the Marshall kids to return home. The neighbour's yard likely had similar paths etched in their lawn. The trail leading to where he stood looked recently used. The grass looked freshly compressed, like it hadn't sprung back up to reach for the sun.

His radio came to life with Harvey's voice.

"The Marshalls are pulling into their driveway. Finkle and Gordon are right behind. Worst tail ever."

"Thanks for the heads up. Give me a couple more minutes."

Max's head jerked skyward at the sound of an approaching chopper. *You better find a lead soon, Maxie boy*, he said to himself. The agent jogged toward the gate and opened it. His assumption about paths proved correct. He followed the one beside the house to the sidewalk on the neighbouring street. Max looked down the street to his right. Nothing. He looked to his left. He thought he spotted a few kids walking away from his position.

His radio crackled again.

"Anything, Max?"

"Maybe," he replied on the radio. "Is that our chopper?"

"Yes. What do I tell them?"

"Have them check the Marshalls' street and the one behind, heading west from their home. They're looking for the Marshall kids. The boy should have a noticeable limp."

"How'd you know the kids weren't with the parents in their car?"

"I wouldn't have let Finkle follow them alone otherwise. The boy wasn't with them when they left. He's the key to all of this."

"Are you coming back to the car?"

"No, let's let Finkle think he scared us off. You come to the street behind the house to pick me up. I think we're getting close."

39 On the Run

"Bubbles!" Lindsay called to them as they trailed slightly behind her. "You better get about ten metres off the ground to avoid detection." Watching them move skyward, her head swivelled upward to the right at an approaching rumbling sound – helicopter blades. "Hold off on that!" she called out to the Bubbles.

"What are we going to do, Lindsay?" Benjay asked excitedly.

"They haven't spotted us yet," Lindsay calmly replied.

"We can't hide from a helicopter!" Sarah responded.

"Want to bet? They can't just land that thing anywhere. Once they do see us, it will likely take a few minutes for those agents to get to our location."

"We'll never make it to the fairgrounds before they catch us," Benjay said. "I'm too slow."

"That's exactly my plan, little bro. You and your girlfriend will become our decoy. They're most likely looking for you – and you're easier to pick out due to your limp. From up in the sky, they may mistake Sarah for me." She pulled off her pink cap, handing it to Sarah. "This might make it look more convincing."

"Thanks," Sarah replied. "From a distance it might fool them."

"That's a brilliant plan, Lindsay," Benjay smiled, much more hopeful of a positive outcome. He held out his drawstring bag. "Take some of the snacks. Sarah and I will head away from the fairgrounds. Hopefully, we'll draw the super-spy types away from you and the Bubbles."

"You got it. You've got to look like you're in a hurry. If they call from the helicopter and order you to stop, keep moving. When they get close, double up on Sarah's bike. Make them chase you. They're not going to shoot a couple of kids. Don't let the helicopter stop you - make them catch you with people on the ground, okay?"

Benjay nodded to his sister. "You keep Peepers and the others safe for me."

"Will do. Now get going!"

As Benjay and Sarah headed off, Lindsay called the Bubbles close to her.

"I'm going to need for you to keep close together, and as close to me as you possibly can. If the helicopter flies overhead, you'll have to immediately land at my feet. They can't see three dampeners flying by themselves. It will have to look like I'm trying to carry them."

"Got it," Peepers replied. "Anything we can do? Do you want us to take out the helicopter?"

"What?" Lindsay questioned.

"Knock it out of the sky. We can do that," Brawny answered. "I'm really strong."

"No. I don't want to hurt the pilots."

"We don't have to make it crash, just make it land," Peepers replied.

"I think it's too risky."

Lindsay turned to watch her brother and Sarah head back toward the house, putting some distance between them. She looked at the dampeners bobbing down the street, the Bubbles in clear mode. Lindsay knew anybody driving by would do a double take at the seemingly floating poles. She had to think fast. An idea came to mind as a nearby shopping centre came into sight.

"You guys need to hide behind this hedge over here. You can set the dampeners down for a bit to get a rest." She pointed nearby and watched them settle onto the grass. "I'll come right back."

Lindsay found a shopping cart abandoned near the road, far from the shopping centre. She grabbed it firmly by the handles and swung it around to face the nearby hedge. Pulling in front of the Bubbles, she instructed them to place two dampeners

185

at the back of the cart closest to the handle, and one near the front. She told Fret to sit in the middle and hold the front pole to keep it from falling back with the cart's movement.

"That's awesome," Shine replied, relieved at no longer having to carry the device. "Is it okay if I sit in there with Fret? I can make sure the other two don't move."

"It may be a tight fit," Lindsay said.

"It will be cozy," Shine smiled, snuggling up to her boyfriend in the cart.

"Alright, let's go!" Peepers proclaimed.

Lindsay pushed the cart, now looking like she moved her purchases down the street.

40 Catch Me if You Can

Benjay and Sarah retraced their route back toward his house. A block away, Benjay asked her to stop.

"You know what we need?" Benjay asked.

"We need a plan," they said simultaneously.

They laughed.

"You first," Benjay requested.

"My dad is always telling us to think a few steps ahead about what outcomes could result from each step. He compares it to chess, but I'm just learning how to play."

"I get it," Benjay replied excitedly. "If we walk down the street in front of our house, the spy guys could jump out and catch us. I run too slow."

"Exactly," Sarah smiled. "But if we walk down the street to draw their attention, then hop on the bike, we can get away from them."

"Up to the point they get in their cars to chase us," Benjay added. "Then we have to get off the streets where they

187

can't follow us – we can head onto the trails in the conservation area!"

"Perfect! They can't drive in there – the trails are too narrow. I didn't see the agents had motorcycles."

"What's next?" Benjay asked.

"Well," Sarah twirled her hair, thinking. "The helicopter might not have the ability to track us precisely from above, but they'll have someone waiting for us at the other end of the trail."

"We could just loop around the trails."

"We could, if you think it will buy us enough time for Lindsay to get to the fairgrounds. But I think we should have another plan for getting out of the park."

"Yeah, I guess you're right." Benjay had no hair to twirl while thinking. He tugged on his right ear a few times instead. "What about the culvert?"

"That's brilliant, Benjay! Assuming they're waiting at the end of the trail, riding through the culvert will veer us off sharply. It will bring us out on a different street. And they'll have to drive all the way around the water treatment site to get to us!" She leaned over and gave Benjay a hug. She pulled back to see his blushing face, which in turn made her blush.

"Uhm," she cleared her throat. "Are you ready?"

"I'm always ready for adventure," Benjay replied, trying to convince himself as much as assure her.

They walked down the street, trying to look engaged in casual conversation, but looking around frequently for activity

188

on the street. Walking a few houses down from Benjay's house, they saw his front door open. Two men also emerged from a car parked in front of the Marshalls' neighbour. Behind them, they could hear the approaching helicopter.

"I think now would be a good time to get on the bike," Benjay said to Sarah.

"Let's wait a minute," she answered.

"You do remember it takes a few seconds for me to climb up on the handlebars and for you to get the bike up to speed?" Benjay replied, more excitement in his voice.

"You're right," she said looking around. "As soon as we get on the bike, they're going to start running this way. Move in front of the bike first."

Benjay did so, shifting the bag he carried to the front to make it easier to jump on the handlebars. She hopped on her bike. Sure enough, the agents began running at them. Benjay hopped up. Sarah began pedalling as fast as she could. Benjay looked over his shoulder.

"They're gaining on us, Sarah!" He could feel the bike's speed increasing. Would it be fast enough, he wondered?

Sarah didn't reply, instead bearing down on the mission at hand.

"That's it, Sarah! We're pulling away from them."

"Thankfully," Sarah gasped. "My legs are burning from pedalling that hard!"

"You were amazing," he told her. "For a few seconds, I thought they'd catch us."

"Off to the park, right?" Sarah started to say but her voice disappeared into a loud roar overhead.

A black military looking helicopter lowered in front of them, hovering about fifty metres off the ground.

"CHILDREN – STOP WHERE YOU ARE!" boomed a voice from the metal hovering beast.

Frankly, it scared both Sarah and Benjay. Neither said anything – it would have proved pointless with the whirling blades drowning out everything, even encroaching on their thoughts.

Sarah stuck to plan. She put her hand on Benjay's right hand that clutched the handlebars, hoping he got the hint to hang on. She could see him tighten his grip. The young girl turned the bike as sharply as she could, hoping Benjay could hold on and that they didn't wipe out in a horrible spill. For a split second, she felt the bike teetering from poor weight distribution. Benjay leaned away from the turn, steadying the wheeled craft. Sarah put her foot to the floor, so to speak. The bike began to speed away from the chopper. Coming straight toward her drove three black sedans. Adrenaline flowing, she powered the bike around the corner onto a short side street that led to the conservation area. Behind her came the sound of the sedans' squealing tires as they sped around the corner after her. Sarah peered around

190

Benjay, gauging the distance to the four metal poles blocking vehicle access to the park. It'd be close.

Benjay looked ahead. Almost there, he sighed to himself. He glanced over his left shoulder at their pursuers. He didn't have to turn far. One of the black sedans pulled up beside them, lowering the window. The passenger yelled at them to stop. Benjay knew the next move would be to cut them off. They had almost no chance of getting to the park before that happened. He had to do something. He removed one hand from the handlebars, reached into his bag and pulled out an apple. In the same motion, he hurled the apple at the open window. The passenger in the car ducked, resulting in the flying apple striking the driver in the right arm. The driver jerked the wheel of the car, coming within inches of striking the handlebars of the bike. Fortunately, he yanked the wheel back the other way. The car swerved over the curb, onto the sidewalk, and struck a small tree on the front lawn. Sarah raced between the barricade poles into the safety of the park.

41 Laying a Trap

Max pounded his fists on the exploded airbag in front of him. He really wanted to beat on his partner, Harvey.

"What were you thinking back there?" Max asked.

"I wasn't. It's instinct. You get an object thrown at you, you duck!" Harvey replied.

"You must have sucked at baseball," Max laughed.

Harvey laughed back.

"Now what?" Harvey asked.

"Can you ride a bike better than catch?"

"What are we going to do – chase them on bikes?"

"That's precisely what we're going to do." Max turned in his seat to look at Harvey. "I'll bet if you try to radio the chopper right now, you won't get through. Why? I bet Finkle is talking to them to find out where the kids are headed. He plans to catch them at the other end of the park."

Harvey tried the radio but couldn't get through. Per usual, his senior partner knew his stuff. A few seconds later,

Finkle's sedan backed up and peeled away, the other car following behind.

Their radio came on requesting a response. Harvey answered. The chopper gave them a location to wait, in case the kids came out of that entrance. Harvey replied and turned off the radio.

"You know Finkle got the most likely spot and will wait there. The other car got the second most likely. So, our spot is the least likely." Max paused. "Based on the way these kids think, I like our odds."

"What about the bikes?"

"Our destination is in a residential area bordering the conservation area. We'll procure some bikes there."

42 Finding Fret

Faith, Cura, Tempo, and the two Velan guards had already travelled a few hours en route to terminate the signal from Fret's tracking device. The guards kept a few metres back. They wore Destabilizers holstered around their midsections. A small red indicator showed the devices were not ready to fire. Pressing the firing button once armed the weapon and turned the light green. Pressing a second time fired the weapon. Cura carried a Destabilizer at his side instead of wearing it.

"Tempo," Faith stated, "you should head to the Bulle globe now. Tell Justice the situation."

"Will do," Tempo replied. "I enjoyed meeting you, Cura."

Cura nodded.

Tempo began to move away but Faith called to her to wait.

Faith looked around to make sure the guards did not follow.

"Listen," she whispered. "Tell Justice about the Destabilizers. I recommend that no other Bulle be sent to the surface. If this whole thing goes wrong, I want as few casualties as possible." She stared intensely into Tempo's eyes. "And give Hope an update. I'm sure she's worried."

Tempo nodded. "I'll get your message to him as quickly as I can. And to Hope. Don't worry." She flew off like a shot.

A few hours later, Cura asked the remaining members of the party to stop.

"Are you tired, Cura?" Faith asked.

"A little – I don't get off Globe much. It takes my body longer to adjust to breathing the different air." He smiled. "And I'm not as young as I used to be, though I never could fly like Tempo," he laughed. Cura flipped over the Destabilizer. He'd attached another small device to the back.

"What's that?" Faith inquired.

"Humans have trackers. I have a Bubble tracker."

"Really? It tracks Bubbles?"

"Yes. We have a few unique chemicals in our bodies that I've learned to trace. Devising a way to detect those at any useful distance proved tricky."

"How far away can a Bubble be?"

"Ten kilometres, give or take."

"Ten kilometres? That's amazing. You're amazing," she grinned. "That little gizmo can save us a lot of time trying to find Fret and the others."

"That's the hope." Cura activated the device. Nothing showed up on the small screen.

"Are we too far away still?"

"Maybe. It takes time for the scan to happen. Five minutes should tell us if we're in range."

Faith moved in close, pretending to look at the tracker. She whispered, "What about these guards? What's your plan for them?"

"I'll keep my eyes on them."

"Aren't they supposed to guard you?" Faith asked.

"Absolutely not."

"But Cage said …"

"Cage was blowing smoke."

"Then what are they here for?"

"They're here to test the Destabilizer on humans."

"What?!" Faith exclaimed, quickly looking over her shoulder to see if the guards reacted to her yelp.

"Cage doesn't do anything out of the kindness of his heart, assuming he has one. He needs a field test to convince the other Elders to build enough Destabilizers to outfit an army."

"We can't let that happen," Faith stated.

The Bubble tracker screen suddenly flashed a green dot. Then another. Then some more.

"How many Bubbles did you say you had on the surface?" Cura asked.

"Five," she replied. "Fret, Peepers, Shine, Change, and Brawny."

Cura pointed at the screen, where a group of dots appeared huddled together.

"I count five dots in that group," Cura said. A puzzled look came across his face. He lowered his voice, to avoid the guards hearing him. "One of those five dots is blue. Have you got a Morph on the surface?"

"Yes, Change is a Morph. Why?" she asked, knowing full well the prejudice of some prominent Vela Elders.

"It's no concern to me," Cura replied, "but the guards holding the Destabilizers might not feel the same."

"Concern noted," she said, glancing over her shoulder at them. "I'm watching them close anyway." She looked back down at the device. "Are you sure this tracker is accurate?" Faith questioned.

"We've tested the device pretty thoroughly," Cura replied.

"So, what are these two green dots?"

She pointed to a dot not too far from the cluster, and another at the far edge of the screen, perhaps seven or eight kilometres away.

43 Buying Time

Deep into the conservation area, Sarah slowed the bike to a stop. Benjay jumped off, rubbing his butt.

"A little numb," he apologized.

Sarah laughed. "I thought maybe the bump going over that last bridge did it." She hopped off and did the same. She looked up to see the chopper blades in the distance between the tree branches overhead. "How much time have we killed?"

Benjay looked at his watch. "Twenty minutes. Need ten minutes more for Lindsay to get settled at the fairgrounds."

"I say we sit here for five minutes to rest. My legs are killing me."

"I'm sorry that I can't pedal very good yet."

"No problem," she smiled. "I'll feel fine in a few minutes. We've almost made it." She gave him an encouraging rub on the shoulder.

"Thanks for your help," he responded. "The Bubbles appreciate it too."

"They are so cool!"

"I'm surprised you believed me."

"I trust you, Benjay Marshall." She smiled. "We make a good team, don't we?"

Before he could agree, the chopper sounds got closer.

"I think it's time to go," Benjay said, looking up at the closing chopper.

"I suppose, but they've got nowhere to land."

As they looked up, the door of the chopper slid open. A man leaned forward with a rifle.

"This way," Sarah hollered. "Under the trees!"

They heard something strike a nearby tree as they scampered under cover. Benjay looked back to see a dart-like object protruding from the trunk.

"Tranquilizer, I think," he said to Sarah.

She sat on the bike. "Get on! I'm going to ride as close to the tree line as possible. The entire trail has cover about thirty metres ahead. Once we get there, we should stay safe until we veer over to the culvert."

Sarah navigated the bike to the edge of the path, slowly picking up speed. She weaved slightly, in case of another shot from above, all the time trying to hug the tree line to reduce the odds of getting hit. Nearing the tree canopy ahead, she darted from the right of the trail to the left side. She felt something whiz by her right shoulder. Ahead, a branch of a small tree exploded as the projectile snapped it into two.

"Holy!" Benjay hollered, instinctively ducking.

Sarah pedalled a few more hard strokes then let up, having reached the cover of large trees.

"Did you see that?" Benjay shouted back to her.

"I felt it!" she exclaimed. "It whistled right past my shoulder. If that had hit me, it would have knocked me right off the bike. They do know we're kids, don't they?"

"How far to the culvert?" he asked.

"Just up here. The side trail to the culvert splits off under the canopy. Hopefully, they assume we stay on the main trail. That will give us time to get through the culvert."

"I'll keep a lookout above."

"Here we go," Sarah said. "It's going to get bumpy on the side trail. The dirt bikers have built up some obstacles."

As she turned, they immediately encountered a sharp dip, followed by a small hill. The bike went airborne, dropping hard to the ground.

"Ouch," Benjay shouted.

A sharp bank turn came next, followed by another, and then another.

"Sorry I can't slow down," Sarah called to him. "I'm afraid I won't make all the hills if I do."

Just then came another dip and hill, followed by an even higher flight from the ground. An 'umph' followed from Benjay as the bike came back to earth. As Sarah coasted for a few seconds, they heard voices ahead. She didn't know what to expect, with all the obstacles ahead.

"What do you see, Benjay?"

"Looks like a couple of those agents on bikes, blocking the path around the next bend."

"I'm going to have to go around them – hold on!"

Sarah picked a smallish opening in the bushes. She barrelled through it, leaving the trail behind. Branches scraped Benjay as they whipped by. She looked beside her to see the men startled at her crazed attempt to avoid them. She spotted another opening, swerving through it back onto the path. She sped the bike through a series of dips, jumps, and curves until the trees peeled back to expose the culvert. The small creek had a foot wide cement ledge on each bank, with rocks held together in wire mesh up the sides. She had to ride extremely near the water's edge to prevent hitting her pedal on the wire mesh. Benjay began to turn to look back to see if the men followed.

"Don't turn around!" Sarah yelled out. "I'm afraid I'll lose balance if you shift your weight. Let me do it."

Rolling under the roadway above, she glanced back at her pursuers. They trailed by about thirty metres. The older guy in front seemed to close on them. The younger guy behind struggled on a bike much too small for his adult frame. She knew the guy in front would catch them shortly, but they should have bought the needed time by then.

"Hold on, Benjay. There's a path up the embankment right after we exit the tunnel."

202

She coasted for a few seconds, knowing she'd lose ground to her pursuers but needing a quick breather prior to attacking the steep hill ahead. She turned onto the path, put her head down, and siphoned all her energy into pedalling as hard as possible. To her dismay, they flew up the hill and neared the top very quickly. She glanced back.

"Stop!" screamed Benjay.

His yell came too late.

Their bike slammed into a black sedan parked at the top of the hill. The front tire hit the car. Benjay flew hard into the passenger side window, crumpling in a heap on the ground. The sudden stop propelled Sarah over the car. Her right shoulder banged off the top of the car on her descent. She continued unrestrained to the road on the other side. The crack of her skull on the concrete emitted a wretched sound.

Max jumped off his bike, letting it roll to the ground. He ran straight to Benjay, who he could see lying at the passenger door. As Max knelt, Benjay began to sit up.

Harvey arrived a few seconds later.

"Call 9-1-1!" Max barked at his partner. "Medical emergency."

Harvey went around to the driver's side of the car, the passenger side inaccessible.

"Max! You better get over here. We've got a bleeder!"

Max propped up Benjay, who had no external signs of injury, patted his shoulder, and ran to the other side of the car. He took off his jacket to prop up Sarah's head.

"Pop the trunk, Harvey. I need the medical kit."

Harvey pushed the trunk release in mid-sentence while talking to the 9-1-1 dispatcher.

Max flung the kit onto the ground next to Sarah's body. He frantically rifled through the contents to find medical wipes, gauze, and a bandage wrap. He wiped at her skull, clearing fragments of asphalt and dirt from the wound. He applied gauze, though blood continued to freely pour out. He knew it was bad. Really, really bad. He wrapped the wound and applied pressure, holding the girl tightly in his arms. He could feel her breaths weaken.

Benjay staggered around the front of the car, using the hood for balance. Upon seeing Sarah, he rushed to her side. Reaching her, she gasped for a breath, her body lurching. Then she stopped breathing.

44 Fairgrounds

Lindsay stopped in her tracks.

"What's the matter?" asked Peepers.

"Oh, likely nothing," Lindsay answered. "It just …"

"Just what," the Bubble asked.

"I just got a feeling. When Benjay's in trouble, sometimes I get a feeling. It's hard to explain."

"No need to," Peepers replied. "We often get similar feelings about siblings."

"It's not very common in people."

"What do you think is wrong with Benjay?"

"I can't tell. Just that something is wrong."

"I'm sure he's fine," Peepers reassured her. "He's a tough little guy."

"I suppose," Lindsay replied. She paused for a few more seconds. "I guess we should get on with our task at hand – getting into the fairgrounds."

"Where's the entrance?" Shine asked.

"We can't just stroll through the entrance."

205

"Why not?" asked Fret.

"Well, first, we need money. I have a couple of dollars but not enough for a ticket. Besides, I can't go waltzing in there with this shopping cart."

"What's a waltz?" Brawny questioned.

"It's a type of dance old people do," Lindsay answered.

"Why would we dance like old people to get into the park? You humans have some strange customs," Peepers remarked.

"It's an expression. It means walking in like you don't have a care in the world."

"Oh," the Bubbles all replied.

"Any ideas how we can get in?" Lindsay asked.

"We could all merge, make a giant bubble, and pull you through the fence," Change offered.

"You can do that?"

"Yes, but," Change added, thinking about it more, "I don't think we could carry the dampening poles too – too much weight. Merging and going through things takes a lot of energy."

"We have to keep Fret inside the dampeners until we reach the right ride."

"We could carry you and the cart over the fence," Peepers suggested.

"That should work," Brawny added. "If we find a remote spot, we won't need to go invisible either."

All the Bubbles agreed to the plan. Lindsay pushed the cart around to the side of the fairgrounds. She found a spot that looked good.

"Get in the cart with Fret," Change told Lindsay.

"I'm a little big to sit in a shopping cart!" she protested.

"It's the only way we can carry you over," Change responded.

Lindsay nodded and squeezed in, holding Fret on her lap.

The remaining Bubbles each took a corner to lift the cart. On a count of three, they lifted. Lindsay felt like she was flying – probably because she and the shopping cart had become airborne. Straight up they went, parallel to the fence. Above the top, they slowly moved forward. Almost completely over, Peepers let her corner lower without noticing. The back wheel caught on the fence, plunging the cart to the ground. The dampening poles flew in different directions, two of them smashing on the ground. Lindsay landed with a thud, fortunately on her rear end. She dusted herself off and stood up.

"We need to hurry – every second until we get to the ride means a second that they can track Fret."

45 Tears

"Where's that ambulance!" Max shouted rhetorically to his partner out of frustration. He'd moved Sarah away from Benjay and lay her flat, administering CPR. He continued for five minutes, pausing only to look for signs of paramedics.

"Max," Harvey said softly to his partner after checking for a pulse.

"Not now, Harvey. I'm busy."

"Max," he said firmly, but not shouting. "It's too late."

"It can't be ..."

"Max," Harvey repeated, his arm on his partner's shoulder. "It's time to let go."

Max wept on bended knee as he picked up Sarah, cradling her in his arms. Looking at the distraught boy beside him, he carefully passed her limp body over to Benjay to hold.

Benjay whimpered a 'thank you' as he held her head close to his chest. Tears flowed from his cheeks onto hers. He closed his eyes. He thought of how much she had impacted his life in the brief time he'd known her, especially over the past few days. As he held her close and thought only of her, something strange happened. It felt like energy leaving his body, moving into hers. At first it startled him. Then he let it happen. Though he could feel his body weaken, he could feel his spirit lift. He felt happiness like he'd never felt before. Then he passed out.

Twenty minutes later, Benjay awoke inside an ambulance.

"Take it easy, kid," Max told him. "You're going to be okay."

"Sarah…" he asked.

"I don't know what you did, kid, but look for yourself."

Benjay turned the other way. Sarah sat cross-legged on the other gurney, smiling at him. She had a small scrape on her forehead but otherwise looked unharmed.

"But you were …"

"Dead. Yes, the agents here told me. It just felt like a nap to me. They told me that you saved me, somehow. How'd you do it, Benjay?"

Benjay just stared. "I have no idea. I just wanted you to be better."

"We're taking you both in for observation. Have the real doctors check you out," Max stated. He turned to the paramedics to apologize. "No offence meant."

Max's phone rang. Seeing the caller ID, he answered. "Yeah?"

"Max, it's Harvey."

"I know, Harvey. What's up?"

"The Detector 2000 went off for a spell. We got a signal for about five minutes then it went dead again."

"Where at?"

"The fairgrounds, northeast corner," Harvey told him.

"The fairgrounds," Max repeated loud enough for Sarah and Benjay to hear. "Based on the expression on these kids' faces, you've got the right place." He looked at his watch. "Meet me at the fairgrounds' main entrance. I'm going to divert the ambulance there. Hold on a sec." He put his phone to his chest to yell up to the driver. "Change of plans. Since these kids both seem okay, we're going to the fairgrounds. How much longer?"

The driver spoke into his radio, "Give me a minute." He muted the radio, pressed the intercom, and replied to Max. "Fifteen minutes, Detective." The driver released the intercom to return to his radio. "Yes, that's right. He said the fairgrounds."

46 Haunted House

Finkle had contacts throughout the force as well as in many of the departments with whom he did business on a weekly basis. Some of them may have mistakenly thought of Finkle as a friend. To the detective, these were purely business relationships. Whenever he did anyone a favour, he expected it returned, with interest. Some of his contacts accused him of extortion – he much preferred the term leverage. The paramedic driving the ambulance, Jimmy, was more than happy to pass information onto Finkle to get back a few unfortunate photos of him sleeping on the job in the ambulance.

"That Jimmy's a good guy, isn't he?" Gordon said to Finkle, hearing about the tip on the fairgrounds but not knowing the backstory.

"Oh, yeah," Finkle grinned. "Jimmy's the best."

"We'll get to the fairgrounds at least five minutes ahead of Max and Harvey. Do you think the thing will still be in the northeast corner?"

"Likely. It's hiding. Probably found what it thinks is a safe place and is laying low."

"Makes sense," Gordon responded.

"Weren't you at the fairgrounds last week?" Finkle asked his partner.

"We were. I blew a small fortune winning a large stuffed rabbit."

"Loser," Finkle laughed. "What's in the northeast corner?"

Gordon thought for a few seconds. "Let's see. I think there are three rides back there. The Ferris wheel, sack slides, and haunted house. Oh yeah, and a few food trucks. I got a giant pretzel there – it tasted sooo good!" He bit his tongue as the last comment came out – he knew Finkle hated small talk.

Finkle shook his head at his partner. "If it's me, I'm hiding in the haunted house. It's the only place you can really hide amongst the things you listed."

"Makes sense. Are you still thinking stun guns?"

"That crazy Dr. Kane contained them with electricity. No reason we shouldn't be able to do the same."

"What's the plan? Get the operator to clear the ride and stop it? We head in, one from the start and one from the end." Gordon reiterated standard operating procedures to reduce the risk of civilian harm.

"No, we can't risk spooking this thing off, pardon the pun. It will know something's wrong if the ride stops for ten minutes. But we can stop sending in new people, then I'll I go in that way. You can start at the end of the ride to traverse your way upstream, as it were."

"You're the boss."

"And don't forget it," Finkle replied.

Finkle and the fairgrounds manager stood talking to the young haunted house ride operator. While the cars for the ride kept moving, the line of people stopped flowing. Many of the waiting riders groaned watching the operator put a chain across the entrance.

"It will only take a few minutes, folks. Just running a spot inspection. Nothing to worry about."

An anxious buzz about a possible accident began in the crowd. The sign of other riders safely exiting the ride calmed them down.

The fairgrounds manager equipped Finkle and Gordon with brightly coloured vests with the word 'safety' emblazoned in large yellow letters across the back.

Finkle boarded a car; Gordon stood at the ready by the exit. The small, haunted house car carrying Finkle slipped through a black slit curtain into the awaiting man-made horrors. Finkle quickly yanked off the safety vest, grumbling as he tossed it against the wall that he knew stood there but couldn't see. Lights flashed and thunder roared as tombstones spookily appeared on the right. The car turned slightly toward the

215

headstones before jolting hard to the left. A pair of glowing skeletons appeared out of nowhere, accompanied by scary moaning. 'Not bad,' Finkle thought to himself. He could imagine the sounds of shrieking kids. He pulled out his flashlight to look for the hidden doors used to service the ride. The alien had to have hidden somewhere behind one of the doors or someone would have spotted it. The ride operator had noted the building had five doors, though Finkle didn't believe much in trusting kids when it came to recalling details. Supposedly only one of the doors could access the ride from the exterior of the building. The kid swore he'd locked it twenty minutes ago, after his break. The ride stood two floors tall, with three hidden doors on the main floor, including the exterior exit. After a trio of holographic ghosts flew in front of his ride, Finkle jumped out. His light illuminated a door. Apparently, the holographic display needed frequent attention, warranting nearby service access. The door creaked upon opening it. He felt around the wall for a light switch. Looking around he found the holographic projector. It fired up again for the next passing car. With no signs of anything out of place, Finkle flicked off the switch, closed the door, and hopped into the nearest car.

Gordon kept his flashlight on, pointing to the ground as he walked. Tracing the ride in reverse proved trickier than he thought. Though he could hear oncoming cars, he had no concept of the gap. The ride snaked around the rectangular box where it

216

made its home. He knew about six or seven more cars had riders making their way through the winding, dark maze. Though he didn't want to spoil the ride for any of them, more importantly he didn't want to get run down. A few of the curves barely had room for a car to fit through, let alone him to stand safely to the side. Gordon looked for those sections, scurrying through them to the next wider section. Getting to the second floor also proved a challenge. Seeing the ramp for the first time, he scrambled toward a wall as a car with four screaming riders plummeted toward him. His choice of direction proved poor though. A mechanical headless man carrying his bloodied head shot out from the wall, striking Gordon firmly. The contact sent him to the ground amid a shrill of shrieks out of the riders. Dazed, he jumped out of the way just in time as the headless man returned to the wall, waiting for the next car of victims. Catching his breath, he sat with his back pressed firmly against the wall. Gordon counted until the next car shot by him. Knowing he had twenty-five to thirty seconds, Gordon headed up the ramp. He first tried the right side but found no footholds. A quick flash of his light revealed some tread strips on the left side. He flashed up the ramp, knowing time had almost run out. At the top, he stepped back and up onto a ledge out of the path of the oncoming cars and next group of riders. Hearing a car approach, he didn't illuminate the area with his light. Clinging to the wall, a sudden flash of light blinded him. His body propelled forward. He raised his hand over his eyes to protect himself from the glare and

217

instinctively yelled. Nearby, he heard four teens screech. He'd apparently stopped on a moving platform that lunged him with two cadavers in front of the ride just prior to the car hurtling down to the main floor. The kids likely pissed their pants at how lifelike the body in the middle appeared.

Gordon stopped to catch his breath – and regain his eyesight. He knew he couldn't wait long though with another car approaching. He flashed his light around the area, pleased to see a door not more than six feet away. He bolted for the door and hurried inside. Closing the door quickly, he leaned up against it, facing outside to catch his breath and listen. Gordon heard the next car go by, though the screams seemed subdued by comparison. He breathed a sigh of relief. Then a thought struck him. The light was on in this room. He turned quickly. His jaw dropped to the floor.

47 Second Place

Max and Harvey couldn't believe it. How did any officers get to the haunted house ahead of them? Obtaining the description of the agents from the fairgrounds manager, Max cursed Finkle under his breath.

"How long since they went inside?" Max inquired.

The manager replied, "Maybe ten minutes?"

"Eight minutes and thirty seconds," the operator replied. Each car is thirty seconds apart. We let eight go before the detective, he got in one, and eight more since." He looked at the ride. "Nine minutes when this next car leaves."

Max looked at the operator. "Good attention to detail, kid. Anything else you can tell us?" The operator described the access doors inside the ride, including more detail than he had to Finkle about what lay behind each door. As Max and Harvey donned their safety vests, Max turned to his younger partner.

"Did you hear that?"

"What?"

"I talked to the fairgrounds manager. He said that kid gave us twice as much information as he gave Finkle."

"And your point is?"

"I just gave the kid a little praise in front of his boss. He opened right up."

"Maybe you can try that in our office," Harvey replied, smiling.

"Ouch!" Max feigned a grimace. "Just last week, I told our boss that you weren't the worst detective that I ever worked with."

Harvey clipped on the vest and laughed. "Wow, that's an amazing compliment. I'll likely get a promotion from that alone."

"Hey, at least I put you ahead of Finkle." Max laughed. "And we'll both get ahead of Finkle in finding the Bubble. From what the kid told me, our best bet is to enter through the exit. The room at the top of the plunge is the most likely place for the thing to hide. The crew rarely goes in there. They don't service any ride functions from there. The other rooms get accessed every few hours for routine maintenance."

"Anything else?"

"Yeah, he said stay to the left going up the ramp or you're bound to find yourself attacked by a headless axe-wielding man."

48 What are You?

Gordon stared in disbelief. In the middle of the room, five balloon like objects floated in midair. Five balloon like objects with *eyes*. Eyes that stared at him. Or should he say through him. The eyes felt like they penetrated his skin.

"What are you?" Gordon stammered to say. He raised his stun gun in defence.

"How many more of you are there here?" one of the orbs asked.

"You can talk?"

"How many more humans are after us?"

"Just one more. For now," Gordon replied.

The alien signaled another, which flew off through a wall. Other aliens restrained a much larger alien from charging.

"All we ask is that you leave us alone a bit longer and we will go," the lead alien stated.

"Oh, I can't do that," Gordon replied, the stun gun shaking in his hand. "My boss would not approve."

"And what do *you* think?"

"That doesn't matter."

"Why?" the alien asked.

"I have to follow orders."

"I don't understand," the alien responded. "We understand that humans, especially on this part of the planet, value their rights to make their own decisions."

"It's different in this case. In my job I'm required to follow the orders of my superior officers."

"How is he superior?" the alien asked.

"In rank. He's my boss."

"Interesting. So free will gives way to hierarchy."

"He can't make me do something that I think is wrong," Gordon replied.

"Yet it appears that you are going against your conscience."

Gordon slowly lowered the stun gun to rest beside his leg.

"What are you doing here? On earth?"

"My name is Shine."

"Gordon."

Shine nodded. "Right now, we're waiting to extract the tracking device from my friend.'

"Why don't you just take him back to your ship?" Gordon asked.

"We feared that you would track him back to … our ship."

"Makes sense. You said you're waiting. What are you waiting for?"

"One of our doctors is coming to operate."

"Well, your doctor better get here ahead of my partner. He's going to stun all of you, then turn you into science experiments."

49 Follow the Dots

Apprehension gripped Faith as they neared the location of the five dots on the screen. Now the sixth dot appeared very near the same spot. The seventh dot hadn't moved. Curious, she thought.

"Ready your weapon," the one Velan guard told the other.

"Put those away," demanded Cura. "There's no need for those yet."

"We just want to be ready, doctor," the guard replied. "These humans are violent beings."

"Maybe, but what does it say about us if we go in with weapons drawn?" Cura asked.

The guard grunted disapproval but lowered his weapon then signalled the other to do the same.

"We better change to clear mode now to avoid detection," Faith commented. "I want a low approach to this building ahead to get a better reading of the location of the Bubbles."

Slowly circling the building agitated the guards. Anxious to gather some intelligence on how well the Destabilizers worked, they wanted to test it on one of the humans below. Cura sensed the mounting tension, suggesting to Faith that they better pick an entry point soon or risk losing the guards to an unprovoked attack.

"We'll enter on this side," Faith directed. "Many humans occupy the building, with a bunch of them screaming. We should prepare for the worst." Reluctantly, she added, "You better ready your weapons."

"Finally!" one guard exclaimed, arming his weapon. "Let's see what these babies can do!"

50 Escape

Benjay became fidgety as his strength fully returned.

"How long since they left?" he asked Sarah.

"Maybe ten minutes," she replied. "They told us to stay here. I think it's good to listen to the police, don't you?"

"Yeah," mumbled Benjay, staring at his shuffling feet.

Sarah moved beside him. She gently put two fingers under his chin to raise his eye level. "But?" she said.

"But the Bubbles may be in danger. I know Peepers. I feel this connection to her."

Sarah frowned.

"Not like a girlfriend," he reassured her. "Like a twin, or something. I hear that twins have a weird connection where they can sometimes feel what the other one is feeling even if they're far apart."

"What do your twin senses tell you?"

"That she's in trouble. That they are all in trouble."

Sarah stood. "I guess we need to do something about it." They couldn't see whether the driver remained in the vehicle. Sarah moved slowly to the back door and pushed it open.

"Please close the door," the driver's voice came over the intercom.

Benjay and Sarah both looked toward the front, startled. She closed the door. "I guess there's something up front that tells him the door is open."

"And there's an intercom. He can probably hear what we're saying."

Like their moods, they slumped down on the seats.

Benjay motioned to Sarah for her phone. She handed it to him. He found the music app and played a song – not too loud to arise suspicion, but loud enough hopefully to drown out their whispering.

"We could just make a run for it," Sarah said. "By the time he gets out of the ambulance, we could have at least a good ten metre head start."

Benjay frowned. "You forget how slow I am. Besides, I only got a small glimpse of what's outside when the detective opened the doors. We wouldn't know the best way to get away."

"Can we create a distraction? I could fake an injury. The driver will come back to check on me. When he opens the door, we can escape."

"I'd still have to run away. He'd catch me, no problem," Benjay replied.

"Not necessarily," Sarah continued to whisper. "I have an idea." She scrounged through the supplies inside the ambulance, finding what she needed. "Just follow my lead." She grabbed her cell phone back. "Oh!" she exclaimed loudly. "I love this song! Crank it up!" She turned up the volume on the song and started dancing. "C'mon Benjay," she yelled over the music. "Dance with me."

Benjay did as she asked. The ambulance began bouncing side to side.

"Hey!" hollered the driver over the intercom. "Stop that racket."

The two kids ignored the request.

"Don't make me come back there!" the driver demanded, to no avail.

Sarah motioned to Benjay. They danced back toward the door. She clutched the medical supply box and a spare crutch she'd spotted. She'd use them to defend herself, if needed. They felt the front door slam as the driver left the vehicle to attend to them. A few seconds later, he flung open both doors.

The kids backed up enough to make the driver enter the ambulance. When he stepped in, Sarah ducked under his arm and squeezed by on the right. She jumped to the pavement outside. She turned, grabbed the closest ambulance door, and flung it shut. Benjay was to have done the same on the other side of the driver. Was supposed to. Didn't.

229

With Benjay ducking to go under the driver's arm, the man stuck his knee out to trap Benjay where he stood. The driver wrestled the squirming Benjay, trying to get him planted on the bench seat. Benjay looked past the driver to see Sarah standing outside. Her hand gripped the handle of the second door, ready to close it when Benjay escaped.

If only he could escape, Benjay thought. He resisted the driver's tightening grasp. He looked again at Sarah. The hope seemed to flicker out of her eyes. He closed his eyes to summon all his strength. What happened next, he couldn't explain.

The driver firmly held Benjay on each shoulder blade. Concentrating on getting loose, something weird started to happen to Benjay. His whole body became jelly-like. He squirted free, tumbling out of the ambulance. He got up from the pavement in time to see the driver's stunned expression. Sarah slammed the second door closed. She quickly shoved the spare crutch between the handles to keep the driver from opening the door from the inside.

The kids headed toward the ride in front of them.

"What happened there?" Sarah said. "It looked like you disappeared for a split second and then reappeared on the other side of the driver. Do you know ninja moves or something?"

"I don't know what happened. It felt like my whole body turned to jelly and he couldn't hold onto me anymore."

"I guess it doesn't matter, as long as we got away. Look!" Sarah exclaimed. "The detectives headed into the haunted house. Let's follow them."

.

51 Encounter

Finkle had checked all three doors on the first floor, including confirming the exit door remained locked from the inside; he didn't trust anyone, especially teenagers. His frustration mounted with each unsuccessful search. With the four-seater ride climbing slowly to the second floor, he cursed having let Gordon start with the exit. It just figured that the kid would find the alien first. Finding that thing would prove a feather in his cap. No matter what Gordon said, Finkle would 'fix' the report to give himself credit when the time came. With the car creaking through the dark up the ramp, suddenly an image appeared in front of him. The ghost of an old woman circled above his head.

"Man, some of these are so lifelike," he said aloud. He swatted at the holographic image. It seemed to swerve away from his swing. "What?" he exclaimed, taking another swing. The old woman circled around, heading straight for him. Her pale, flaking skin and sunken bloodshot eyes sent chills down his spine. Then she flew right through his chest. He instantly felt cold, like something dead had passed through his body. He

233

screamed an ear-piercing high-pitched wail that rattled his own teeth. He jumped out of the moving cart, forgetting it had gone halfway on its uphill climb. Finkle tumbled, his shoulder bouncing off the car with the sound of bone shattering. He yelled in pain as he rolled a few more feet down to the base of the hill. Staggering to his feet, he instinctively grabbed for his ailing shoulder. He'd had a shoulder dislocated playing football. This felt very different – and far worse. Bent over like a hunchback, facing away from the source of the old ghost, he paused to catch his breath. He questioned what he had just seen. Ghosts didn't exist, he told himself. The ride must have released a blast of frigid air to give the sensation he experienced. He'd seen a hologram and trickery, he convinced himself. He'd already conjured up a story about how it happened, too embarrassed by the truth of getting scared on an amusement park ride. Finkle straightened up, rubbing his throbbing shoulder. He'd forgotten that he stood in the centre of the tracks. The next car on the ride emerged from the dark to ram his knees and knock him to the ground with an unceremonious thud. He rolled away from the track to a safe spot to regain his composure.

Making his way back to his feet, he clung to the wall back the way he came, until he saw the daylight of the entrance. Emerging into the bright sunlight, he immediately barked orders at the ride attendant, who had resumed loading riders.

"What are you doing, moron?" Finkle exclaimed. "I gave you orders not to board anyone else."

"The other officer told me I could resume loading riders," the young man replied.

"Why would you be stupid enough to listen to my younger partner when I gave you an order?"

"It wasn't your partner. It was the older detective, Max. He gave me the go-ahead. Said you reported to him."

Finkle cursed under his breath, no longer concerned with the riders. He was far more concerned about his rival arriving on the scene. "Where did this Max guy go?"

The attendant hesitated to respond.

"Come on, dummy. Spit it out."

He pointed at the exit. "They followed your partner."

Finkle nodded, taking a few quick steps toward the exit track. Stopping, he turned and yelled at the attendant. "And no more riders!"

The people in line groaned.

"Look out for …" the attendant stopped in mid-sentence. Why should he alert this jerk to the headless man at the bottom of the ramp? He deserved what he got.

"What, kid?" Finkle hollered.

"Nothing – good luck!"

As soon as Finkle disappeared, the ride attendant resumed loading passengers to a great cheer from those waiting.

52 Out of the Black

Max and Harvey got to the location of the headless man. They paused to get the timing of his movements, per the ride operator's warning.

"You ready?" Max asked his partner.

A sudden commotion behind them cut off Harvey's response. The two kids from the ambulance appeared in the middle of the area.

"Get them, Harv!" Max called out.

An empty car came plummeting down the ramp. The kids both screamed at the sight of the oncoming vehicle, frozen at the edge of the track. Behind them, the headless man began his programmed swing toward the car, on target to knock the kids into its path. Harvey lunged, yanking the screaming girl to the safety of the wall where he had huddled. The girl clung to Harvey, shaking from the experience. Harvey looked across the track to Max, who had successfully pulled the boy to safety.

"What are you doing here?" Max asked Benjay.

"We wanted to help," he replied.

237

"How's that working out for you so far?" Max asked sarcastically. "I don't know how you got away from the ambulance driver, but you need to go back. This is a dangerous situation, as you can see."

"I can't do that," Benjay replied.

"What?" Max asked, stunned by the response.

"I don't want you hurting my friends."

"Who says I'm going to?"

"You're going to try to capture them and hurt them, aren't you?"

"No. I mean yes, I plan to capture them. But no, I don't intend to hurt them, just question them." Max paused, something just clicking. "What do you mean 'them'? We're just tracking one bubble-thing. Do you mean there's more of them?"

"Yes, and I think you'll hurt them trying to capture them."

"Listen kid," Max stated firmly. "There are two other detectives likely already with your friends. They will definitely hurt them if we don't get there soon."

"We need to get going!" Benjay replied.

Max looked across to Harvey. "We're bringing them with us, Harv. We don't have time to take them back."

"Okay, boss. After this next car." A few seconds later, another empty car came hurtling by, accosted by the headless guy. When the vehicle passed, the four of them scampered up the ramp into an opening next to the storage room. They caught their breath during the approach of another car, this one occupied. The occupants screamed at the sight of the four of them lurking in the shadows. The riders plunged down toward the awaiting headless guy waving his detached head. More screams followed.

"See, Harvey," Max laughed. "Didn't I say you look scary ugly?"

Harvey laughed as he pulled out his stun gun. Max did the same. He turned to the kids.

"You kids need to stay here until we give you the 'all clear'." He looked intensely into Benjay's eyes. "I mean it, kid. No following. Got it?"

Benjay nodded without objecting. He knew the detective meant it. He watched the detectives position themselves at the door, then enter on the count of three. He and Sarah crept nearer the door after the detectives entered, trying to hear what happened. Suddenly a ride car came around the corner, the lights illuminating them as the riders screamed in fear. The car turned and plummeted down the ramp, resulting in more screams – followed by yelling from a grown man. Benjay looked at Sarah.

"That must be one of the other detectives. We better go inside to tell that Max guy."

Sarah nodded and opened the door for Benjay to enter.

53 Into the Blue

Benjay entered the storage room expecting to see the two detectives and the Bubbles. Instead, darkness shrouded the room. Sort of. The darkness had a weird blue luminescence to it. He looked at Sarah, who clenched his arm. She shrugged her shoulders.

"I can't see anything, can you?" Benjay whispered.

"Not a thing," she replied in a hushed voice. "I can barely see your face. What's with the blue glow?"

"We don't know," came the voice of one of the detectives, startling the two kids. He couldn't have stood more than a few feet away but seemed to shout in the dim void. "I thought I told you guys to stay outside."

"Someone is coming up the ride behind us. We thought you should know."

"Thanks," replied the detective. "Is there anybody else in here?" he loudly called out.

"Yeah, me, Gordon," replied Finkle's partner.

241

"What's with the lights? The switch isn't working."

"They wanted it that way," Gordon replied. "They can see us clear as day in this lighting. It gives them the advantage. They didn't want anyone going off half-cocked shooting."

"You mean like Finkle," Harvey replied.

"Yeah, like Finkle."

"They're here?" Max asked. "How many of them?"

"Five. But they're waiting for their doctor to remove the tracker from the one you shot."

"You make it sound so bad," Max replied.

"Well, it turned out that way. The Bubble can't return home until they get it removed."

"See, Max," Harvey said. "He called them Bubbles too."

Max ignored his partner's comments, instead replying to Gordon. "Where's home?"

"We didn't get that far. But they are amazing creatures. They mean no harm." Gordon paused, trying to see in the darkness. "If your stun guns are out, you should put them away as a sign of good faith."

Max holstered his stun gun. "Do what he says, Harvey."

"Did you bring the kids with you?" Gordon asked.

"They're both here. It's more like they tracked us down. They escaped from the ambulance and followed us. The boy knows stuff about these Bubbles."

"We can't let Finkle capture the Bubbles," Gordon emphatically stated. "He'll turn them into science experiments and pad his pockets."

"Oh no!" blurted out Benjay.

"Benjay? Is that you?" a female voice came from somewhere above.

"Peepers?"

"Yes, it's me."

"Is Lindsay here with you?"

"Yes, your sister is here too. She's safe."

"They talk?" asked a surprised Harvey.

"I told you they're amazing," Gordon replied.

"We need to come up with a plan. One that will keep the three kids out of harm's way," Max stated. "Any ideas?"

"The Bubbles have a plan, back to the darkness and blue glow. Follow my voice and come over here."

The four newest arrivals gingerly made their way in the direction of Gordon's voice, with a few 'ouches' indicating they'd bumped into a table or spare parts of the haunted house ride. Arriving beside Gordon, Benjay felt a familiar hand on his shoulder.

"Lindsay! I'm happy to see ... well, I can barely see you," he said as his sister hugged him.

"What's the Bubbles' plan, Gordon?" Max asked.

"Their doctor will arrive any minute to operate. We will stun Finkle if he comes into the room. When the door first opens, you can make out a silhouette."

"That's their plan?" asked a surprised Max. "Do they know we'll get brought up on charges by internal affairs for intentionally stunning a fellow officer?"

"They don't really care," replied Gordon.

"And you? Don't you care that your career could end by doing that?"

"If it comes to stunning Finkle, I'm prepared to do it. I'll say I missed the Bubble and hit my partner by accident. It's not like I'm shooting him with a real gun."

Max shook his head. "Better you than me, I guess. They'd never buy that story from me, with my history with Finkle."

"How do we know the Bubbles won't harm us?" Harvey asked.

"They don't have weapons. But just in case some of the others arriving do, they are hovering above us right now as a sign of protection."

The group looked up. The air above them still glowed blue.

"The Bubbles are glowing blue!" Benjay exclaimed. "That's cool, Peepers. Can you remain clear or invisible when you change colours?"

"They can become invisible too?" Max asked, bewildered. "No wonder we have had such a tough time tracking you. It's like chasing shadows. One minute you're there, the next, you're not."

Peepers floated down in front of Benjay, becoming visible though remaining mostly blue. Those large eyes opened brightly. She smiled and extended two arms to hug her friend. "I'm glad you made it safely, Benjay. I, I mean we … we were worried about you."

A faint squeak preceded the door flying open. Finkle barged in, stun gun drawn in front of his face.

Gordon raised his stun gun and pointed at Finkle's outline in the darkness.

"Freeze," Finkle yelled, not able to see anything but warning any potential inhabitants.

Before Gordon could fire, two bursts of light flashed from near the ceiling, both striking Finkle simultaneously. In the residual glow of the blasts, they could see the outline of Finkle crumple to the ground, collaborated by the sound of his stun gun clanging on the floor.

The lights came on, revealing the presence of four new Bubbles. Two of them had weapons drawn from their holsters.

"Whoa!" exclaimed Fret. "Don't shoot the other humans."

Peepers, Fret, Brawny, Shine, and Change changed to natural shading to hover in front of the five humans. They prevented weapons fire.

"Can we trust these other humans?" Faith asked Change.

"Yes, I believe we can," he replied.

"Good," Faith said, removing the Destabilizer belt. "I hate weapons. But," she said smiling at Fret. "I am hopeful that this device will fry the transmitter buried in you." She paused. "Maybe fry is a bad choice of words ..."

"Let's say immobilize," Dr. Cura said, chuckling. "I'm Dr. Cura," he introduced himself to Fret. "I'm from the Vela. Pleased to meet you."

"You too," Fret said. "What do you need me to do?"

"Turn to the side for me. I need to get a good look."

Fret complied as everyone else in the room looked on.

"Hmmm," Dr. Cura hummed, passing the detector over the wound. "I detect the outgoing signal." He turned to Faith. "You were right to stop when you did. A fraction deeper would have paralyzed Fret." He handed the detector to one of the guards to hold while he operated. Cura held up his Destabilizer, pressed some buttons on the back side, then held it above the wound again. "That should be the correct setting."

"How long will this take, Doctor?" Shine asked.

"Just a few seconds," he replied. "Can you brace Fret? This might have a bit of kick to it." He looked at Fret again. "Try to stay perfectly still, Fret. I need to get this positioned correctly."

A short burst emitted from the Destabilizer jolted Fret. Shine kept him from moving. He did his best to hide the pain, hoping one blast did the trick.

Cura looked at the guard. "Let me have that detector again, please."

Instead, the guard held up the device and noticed the blue dot on the screen. He yelled to his partner. "There's a Morph here!" They immediately raised their weapons. The guard scanned each Bubble directly. "It's him!" he hollered, pointing at Change. They fired at Change before anyone could object. Fortunately, Change could transform instantaneously. He morphed into a shield, deflecting the weapons fire back toward the shooters. One shot narrowly missed the first guard. The other shot struck the second guard, sending him convulsing across the room into the back wall.

"Enough!" screamed Cura.

The first guard protested. "Morphs are not allowed away from Bulle without an Elder escort."

"What do you think Faith here is?" Cura replied.

"She wasn't with him until just now," the guard snarled.

"Faith came to the surface with him but had to leave to seek our help."

"You shouldn't have left the Morph alone. It's a violation."

247

Cura sighed. "I will explain the reason to the Elders, but feel free to include that in your report at the end of the mission."

The guard nodded, glaring at Change, and reluctantly lowering his weapon.

Dr. Cura grabbed the detector from the guard that sat recovering in the corner. The doctor passed the device over Fret's wound again. "No signal, Fret. They can't track you anymore. You should be safe to return home."

"Great!" Fret gratefully replied. "Because," he turned to smile at Shine. "I've got to get home to plan an event." He moved close to his girlfriend. "If you'll marry me, that is."

54 The End

Max, Harvey, and Gordon knew their reports would have to match, to explain what happened that afternoon in the haunted house. They agreed to no mention of the Bubbles. They would say that whatever they tracked had caught them by surprise, knocking them unconscious.

The three detectives talked briefly with the Bubbles, saying they wished that they could trust the police force and government to do the right thing if the Bubbles came forward. But they knew it wouldn't happen. There were too many Finkles out there either waiting to make a buck or dissect them in the name of medical research. Many people were simply too paranoid or fearful to admit the existence of another intelligent species, and maybe even a superior one at that.

The Bubbles for their part felt thankful that nobody got seriously hurt. Fret would completely heal in time for his future nuptials. The Velan security felt pleased that the Destabilizers proved effective against Finkle. Their satisfaction grew when able to measure the success of a single blast on a human by knocking out Max, Harvey, and Gordon individually. The Velan security propped the three men onto chairs in the storage room, telling Cura he could leave. They would return after discreetly timing how long the humans remained knocked out. Cura nodded, knowing he didn't have much choice, and hoping it resulted in a more favourable report.

The Bubbles agreed it unnecessary to knock out the kids with the Destabilizers.

"I hope to see you soon," Benjay told Peepers.

"Me too," Peepers grinned. "It was very nice to meet you, Sarah. I'm glad Benjay has such a good friend on the surface."

"Please come back anytime," Sarah smiled. "I'd love to get to know you better."

The faint tones of a police siren became audible and increasing in volume.

"We better get out of here," Lindsay said to her brother and Sarah. "We can't be here when the police discover the three detectives. We just need to get home and stick to our story of me finding you and going home after I got you out of the ambulance. Detective Killjoy said the ambulance driver won't say anything – he'll feel too embarrassed to admit two kids trapped him inside his own vehicle."

"Till we meet again, Peepers," Benjay grinned over his shoulder as they exited the room.

Peepers called out after him. "Maybe at Fret's wedding!"

55 The End (Part II)

Thomas Finkle's head felt like someone had put it in a vice and rotated it two turns past tight. His eyes fluttered, trying to open. He reached to rub his eyes open, but his hands couldn't move. Neither of them. Or his legs. His body felt pressed up against somebody else.

He heard a faint rumbling sound grow louder. It sounded like a train coming down the tracks. The noise intensified. He began to panic, thinking perhaps someone had tied him to train tracks. But whom? And why? His mind raced. He'd screwed over a lot of people in the past ten years. It could almost be anybody.

Finkle heard screaming. Sweat poured down his brow. He forced his eyes open through the stream of stinging sweat. It remained mostly dark around him. His eyes slowly adapted. What was this place? It looked familiar ...

Suddenly, a car with screeching passengers emerged from the darkness above his right shoulder. He felt his body thrust in a circular motion toward the oncoming car. Hot spotlights beamed on him as he swung forward. Piercing shrieks, including his own, penetrated every corner of his skull. As the car rumbled past him, taking the screams with it, the platform holding him swung back out of the way, waiting for the next car full of squealing people. He looked down to see himself tied to a mannequin. His right hand was taped to hold onto something – it looked like hair. He could barely lift his hand. Subjected to the bright lights of the cars in the ride, his eyes struggled to adjust between cars. As the next car approached and the lights lit up his body to scare the passengers, he screamed as he could see what he was holding – a detached head! He turned his hand and slumped in relief when he saw it wasn't real. The platform swung him back toward the wall, jostling his stomach as it did. He barely caught his breath before the mechanism triggered his journey back in front of the oncoming vehicles. He felt like he would puke. With nobody able to hear his calls for help over their own screaming, he wondered, would this horror ever end?

The End

A Small Favour

I hope you enjoyed Bubbles on the Run. Can I ask a small favour?

Leaving a review helps authors, especially independent authors like me!

I appreciate every honest review of my work. It only takes a few minutes – it doesn't need to be an eloquent composition, just a few thoughts will help incredibly! Posting to Amazon or any book site would be appreciated.

Thanks for your time!

Dale J. Moore

Benjay and the Magical Bubbles

Book 1

A Story of
Wonder

Book 1.1

Benjay's
Halloween -
A Short Story

Book 1.2

Benjay's
Santa Claus
Parade - A
Short Story

Book 2

Danger at
Christmas

Book 3

Benjay's
Battle

Young
Writer's
Workbook

254

A Story of Wonder
Book One

A boy and his family, magical creatures with special abilities, and environmental crooks.

What if your new best friend was a Bubble – one that talked and flew? How would you get anyone, especially your parents, to believe you?

Seven-year-old Benjay Marshall wishes people treated him normally. He feels normal; he's just missing part of his leg after dealing with cancer. Fueled by an overactive imagination and a humourous way of expressing himself, Benjay's life takes an extraordinary turn due to a chance encounter with a magical Bubble. As he learns more about the Bubbles, the more he realizes his family will think he's simply spinning another tall tale.

With his father in grave danger from crooks sabotaging his environmental project, how does Benjay make his family trust that Bubbles are not only real, but are possibly the *only* chance to save the day?

Benjay's Halloween:

Book 1.1

A missing cat, a broken leg, and scary skeletons!

In this short story, Benjay's excitement for Halloween keeps hitting roadblocks. Will he go trick-or-treating or be stuck at home handing out candy?

A delightful middle-grade short story that captures the magic and excitement of every child's favorite spooky holiday. An entertaining tale blending humor, adventure, and valuable life lessons about resilience and family bonds.?

Benjay's Santa Claus Parade

Book 1.2

Runaway inflatables, substitute Santas, and pandemonium at the parade!

When young Benjay spots his neighbor Mr. Guenther mysteriously floating in mid-air, he's certain he's discovered Santa's secret identity. When disaster strikes at the Christmas parade, with Benjay trapped in the middle of it, will Santa save the day? Is Mr. Guenther really Santa Claus or is there an even more magical explanation?

This heartwarming adventure proves that sometimes the best Christmas magic comes from ordinary people doing extraordinary things.

Danger at Christmas

Book Two

A human boy, a magical Bubble girl, and lives in danger! How far would *you* go to save someone close?

Eight-year-old Benjay Marshall is back for another adventure with the Bubbles!

Having missed Christmas battling cancer the past two years, Benjay is excited to celebrate all the holiday traditions with his family. Happy Christmas activities take a perilous turn with a robbery at the century-old bank where Benjay's mother works.

Benjay's new Bubble friend Peepers has a terrible feeling that her human friend is in danger. Her fears intensify with the ominous vision from a visiting Elder. With a secret motive, the Bubble Elders launch a mission to verify the vision. Peepers and her older brother Fret leave to investigate the curious vision, not knowing the danger they will encounter. All they know are their orders: keep Benjay safe.

Stopping the robbers seems like a monumental task for an eight-year-old boy with a prosthetic leg and his clever twelve-year-old sister. Can Benjay and Lindsay foil the robbery? Can they rescue their mother? Will the Bubbles be able to help?

Danger at Christmas juggles suspense and humour, with the usual dose of mayhem for Benjay and the Bubbles. Sure to be enjoyed by both boys and girls.

Benjay's Battle

Book Three

A devious doctor, a secret laboratory, and a boy in a fight against time. And of course, magical Bubbles!

Benjay faces the biggest challenge of his young life. His magical Bubble friend Peepers has no idea of the danger that lies ahead as she breaks the rules to help her human friend. It's the kind of danger that could impact all Bubbles. Mysterious events unfold, including unexplained improvements in Benjay's condition and strange dreams of a woman who may be more than she appears. Join Benjay and Peepers as they face peril in their latest magical adventure!

Benjay's Battle is a fast-paced adventure that blends elements of fantasy, science fiction, and mystery while exploring themes of friendship, curiosity, and hope in the face of adversity.

259